Penguin Books
The Wind from Nowhere

J. G. Ballard was born in Shanghai of English parents
in 1930 and lived there until he was fifteen. During the
war he was interned by the Japanese in a civilian prison
camp. He was repatriated in 1946, and after leaving
school read medicine at King's College, Cambridge.
His first science fiction story was published in 1956.
From the start he pioneered a new form of science
fiction, and was the originator of the so-called 'New
Wave' that challenged the American science fiction
of the 1950s. He believes that science fiction is the
authentic literature of the Twentieth Century.
His books published in Penguins are *The Drought*,
The Drowned World, and *The Terminal Beach*.
His other books include *Crash* and *The Atrocity
Exhibition*.

GW00686157

J. G. Ballard

The Wind from Nowhere

Penguin Books

Penguin Books Ltd, Harmondsworth,
Middlesex, England
Penguin Books Australia Ltd, Ringwood,
Victoria, Australia

First published in the U.S.A. 1962
Published in Penguin Books 1967
Reprinted 1974

Made and printed in Great Britain by
C. Nicholls & Company Ltd
Set in Intertype Times

Contents

Chapter 1

The Coming of the Dust

The dust came first.

Donald Maitland noticed it as he rode back in the taxi from London Airport, after waiting a fruitless forty-eight hours for his Pan-American flight to Montreal. For three days not a single aircraft had got off the ground. Weather conditions were freak and persistent – ten-tenths cloud and a ceiling of 700 feet, coupled with unusual surface turbulence, savage crosswinds of almost hurricane force that whipped across the runways and had already ground-looped two 707's on their take-off runs. The great passenger terminus building and the clutter of steel huts behind it were clogged with thousands of prospective passengers, slumped on their baggage in long straggling queues, trying to make sense of the continuous crossfire of announcements and counter-announcements.

Something about the build-up of confusion at the airport warned Maitland that it might be another two or three days before he actually took his seat in an aircraft. He was well back in a queue of about three hundred people, and many of these were husbands standing in for their wives as well. Finally, fed up and longing for a bath and a soft bed, he had picked up his two suitcases, shouldered his way through the mêlée of passengers and airport police to the car foyer, and climbed into a taxi.

The ride back to London depressed him. It took half an hour to get out of the airport, and then the Great West Road was a chain of jams. His departure from England, long pondered and planned, culmination of endless heart-searching (not to speak of the professional difficulties involved in switching his research fellowship at the Middlesex to the State Hospital at Vancouver) had come to a dismal anticlimax, all the more irritating as he had given in to the rather adolescent whim of walking out without telling Susan.

Not that she would have been particularly upset. At the beach house down at Worthing where she was spending the summer, the news would probably have been nothing more than an excuse for another party or another sports coupé, whichever seemed the most interesting. Still, Maitland *had* hoped that the final quiet letter of resignation with its Vancouver postmark might have prompted at least a momentary feeling of pique, a few seconds of annoyance, on Susan's part. He had hoped that even the most obtuse of her boy friends would detect it, and it would make them realize that he was something more than her private joke figure.

Now, however, the pleasure of such a letter would have to be deferred. Anyway, Maitland reflected, it was only a small part of the great feeling of release he had experienced since his final decision to leave England. As the taxi edged through the Hounslow traffic, he looked out at the drab shopfront and grimy areaways, the congested skyline against the dark low cloud like a silhouette of hell. It was only 4 o'clock but already dusk was coming in, and most of the cars had their lights on. The people on the pavements had turned up their collars against the hard gritty wind which made the late June day seem more like early autumn.

Chin in one hand, Maitland leaned against the window, reading the flapping headlines on the newspaper stands.

QUEEN MARY AGROUND NEAR CHERBOURG
High Winds Hamper Rescue Launches

A good number of would-be passengers who should have picked up the liner at Southampton had been at the airport, Maitland remembered, but she had been over a week late on her five-day crossing of the Atlantic, having met tremendous seas, headwinds like a wall of steel. If they were actually trying to take off passengers, it looked as if the great ship was in serious trouble.

The taxi window was slightly open at the top. In the angle between the pillar and the ledge Maitland noticed that a pile of fine brown dust had collected, almost a quarter of an inch thick at its deepest point. Idly, he picked up a few grains and rubbed them between his fingers. Unlike the usual grey detritus of metropolitan London, the grains were sharp and crystalline, with a distinctive red-brown colouring.

They reached Notting Hill, where the traffic stream slowed to move around a gang of workmen dismembering a large elm that had come down in the wind. The dust lay thickly against the kerbstones, silting into the crevices in the low walls in front of the houses, so that the street resembled the sandy bed of some dried-up mountain torrent.

At Lancaster Gate they turned into Hyde Park and drove slowly through the windswept trees towards Knightsbridge. As they crossed the Serpentine he noticed that breakwaters had been erected at the far end of the lake; white-topped waves a foot high broke against the wooden palisades, throwing up the wreckage of one or two smashed rowing boats torn from the boathouse moorings on the north side.

Maitland slid back the partition between himself and the driver when they passed through the Duke of Edinburgh Gate. The wind rammed into his face, forcing him to shout.

'29 Lowndes Square! Looks as if you've been having some pretty rough weather here.'

'Rough, I'll say!' the driver yelled back. 'Just heard ITV's gone off the air. Crystal Palace tower came down this morning. Supposed to be good for two hundred miles an hour.'

Frowning sympathetically, Maitland paid him off when they stopped, and hurried across the deserted pavement into the foyer of the apartment block.

The apartment had been Susan's before their marriage

seven years earlier, and she still paid the rent, finding it useful as a pied à terre whenever she came up to London on a surprise visit. To Maitland it was a godsend; his fellowship would have provided him with little more than a cheap hotel room. (Research on petroleum distillates or a new insecticide would have brought him, at thirty-five, a senior executive's salary, but research into virus genetics – the basic mechanisms of life itself – apparently merited little more than an undergraduate grant.) Sometimes, indeed, he counted himself lucky that he was married to a rich neurotic – in a way, he had the best of both worlds. Indirectly she and her circle of pleasure seekers made a bigger contribution to the advancement of pure science than they realized.

'Good trip, Dr Maitland?' the hall porter asked as he walked in. He was working away with a long-handled broom, sweeping together the drifts of red dust that had blown in from the street and clung to the walls below the radiator grilles.

'Fine, thanks,' Maitland told him. He slid his suitcases into the elevator and dialled the tenth floor, hoping that the porter would fail to notice the discrepancy on the indicator panel over the arch. His apartment was on the ninth, but on his way to the airport he had optimistically assumed that he would never see it again. He had sealed his two keys into an envelope and slipped it through the mail slot for the weekly cleaner to find.

At the tenth floor he stepped out, and carried his suitcases along the narrow corridor around the elevator shaft to a small service unit by the rear stairway. A window let out onto the fire escape which criss-crossed down the rear wall of the building, at each angle giving access to the kitchen door of one of the apartments.

Swinging out, Maitland pulled himself through the railings and made his way down to his own landing. Like all fire escapes, this one was principally designed to prevent burglars from gaining access up it, and only secondarily to facilitate occupants escaping down it. Heavy gates six feet high had been erected at each landing and by now had rusted solidly into their casings. Maitland hunched himself against the harsh wind driving across the dark face of the block, watching the lights in the apartments above him, wrestling with the ancient spring bolt. Nine floors below, the mews in the cobbled yard behind the block was deserted. Gusts of dust-laden air were billowing past the single lamp.

Finally dislodging the bolt, he stepped through and closed the gate behind him. A narrow concrete balcony ringed the rear section of his apartment, and he walked past the darkened windows to the lounge doors at its far end. A light coating of dust grated on the tiles below his feet, and his face smarted from the impact of the countless minute crystals.

He had closed everything up before he left, but one of the French windows had never locked securely since Bobby de Vet, an enormous South African footballer who had doggedly trailed after Susan during a tour five years earlier, had collapsed against it after a party.

Blessing de Vet for his foresight, Maitland bent down and slowly levered the bottom end of the window off its broken hinge, then swung the whole frame out sufficiently to withdraw the catch from its socket.

Opening the window, he stepped through into the lounge.

Before he had moved three paces, someone seized him tightly by the collar and pulled him backward off balance. He dropped to his knees, and at the same time the lights went on, revealing Susan with her hand on the wall switch by the door.

He tried to pull himself away from the figure behind him, craned up to see a broadly built young man in a dinner jacket, with a wide grin on his face, squeezing his collar for all he was worth.

11

Grunting painfully, Maitland sat down on the carpet. Susan came over to him, her black off-the-shoulder dress rustling as she moved.

'Boo,' she said loudly, her mouth forming a vivid red bud.

Annoyed for appearing so foolish, Maitland knocked away the hand still on his collar and climbed to his feet.

'Why, if it isn't the prof!' the young man exclaimed. Maitland recognized him as Peter Sylvester, a would-be racing driver. 'Hope I didn't hurt you, Don.'

Maitland straightened his jacket and tried to loosen his tie. The knot had shrunk immovably to the size of a pea.

'Sorry to break my way in, Susan,' he said. 'Must have startled you. Lost my keys, I'm afraid.'

Susan smiled, then reached over to the phonograph and picked up the envelope that Maitland had dropped through the mail slot.

'Oh, we found them for you, darling. When you started rattling the window we wondered who it was, and you looked so huge and dangerous that Peter thought we'd better take no chances.'

Sylvester sauntered past them and lay down in an armchair, chuckling to himself. Maitland noticed a half-full decanter on the bar, half a dozen dirty glasses distributed around the room. It looked as if Susan had been here only that day, at the most.

He had last seen her three weeks ago, when she had left her car to be cleaned in the basement garage and had come up to the apartment to use the phone. As always she looked bright and happy, undeterred by the monotony of the life she had chosen for herself. The only child of the closing years of a wealthy shipping magnate, she had remained a schoolgirl until her middle twenties.

Maitland had met her in the zone of transit between then and her present phase. At least, he always complimented himself, he had lasted longer than any other of her beaux. Most of them were tossed aside after a few weeks. For two or three years they had been reasonably happy, Susan doing her best to understand something of Maitland's work. But gradually she discovered that the trust fund provided by her father supplied her with a more interesting alternative, an unending succession of parties, and Riviera week-ends. Gradually he had seen less and less of her, and by the time she went down to Worthing the rift had been complete.

Now she was thirty-two, and he had recently noticed a less pleasant note intruding into her personality. Dark-haired and petite, her skin was still as clear and white as it had been ten years earlier, but the angles of her face had begun to show, her eyes were now more sombre. She was less confident, a little sharper, the boy friend of the moment was kept more on his toes, thrown out just those few days sooner. What Maitland really feared was that she might suddenly decide to return to him and set up again the ghastly ménage of the months before she had finally left him – a period of endless bickering and pain.

'Good to see you again, Susan,' he said, kissing her on the cheek. 'I thought you were staying down at Worthing.'

'We were,' Susan said, 'but it's getting so windy. The sea's coming in right over the beach and it's a bore listening to that din all the time.' She wandered around the lounge, looking at the bookshelves. Uneasily, Maitland realized that she might notice the gaps in the shelves where he had pulled down his reference books and packed them away. The phonograph was Susan's and he had left that, but most of his own records he had sent on by sea. Luckily, these she never played.

'Tremendous seas along the front,' Sylvester chimed in. 'All the big hotels are shut. Sandbags in the windows. Reminds me of the Dieppe raid.'

Maitland nodded, thinking to himself: I bet you were

13

never at Dieppe. Then again, maybe you were. I suppose it takes nerve of some sort even to be a bad racing driver.

He was wondering how to make his exit when Susan turned around, a sheet of typewritten paper in her hand. He had just identified the familiar red-printed heading when she said:

'What about you, Donald? Where have you been?'

Maitland gestured lightly with one hand. 'Nothing very interesting. Short conference I read a paper to.'

Susan nodded. 'In Canada?' she asked quietly.

Sylvester stood up and ambled over to the door, picking the decanter off the bar on his way. 'I'll leave you two to get to know each other better.' He winked broadly at Maitland.

Susan waited until he had gone. 'I found this in the kitchen. It appears to be from Canadian Pacific. Seven pieces of unaccompanied baggage en route to Vancouver.' She glanced at Maitland. 'Followed, presumably, by an unaccompanied husband?'

She sat down on an arm of the sofa. 'I gather this is a one-way trip, Donald.'

'Do you really mind?' Maitland asked.

'No, I'm just curious. I suppose all this was planned with a great deal of care? You didn't just resign from the Middlesex and go and buy yourself a ticket. There's a job for you in Vancouver?'

Maitland nodded. 'At the State Hospital. I've transferred my fellowship. Believe me, Susan, I've thought it over pretty carefully. Anyway, forgive my saying so, but the decision doesn't affect you very much, does it?'

'Not an iota. Don't worry, I'm not trying to stop you. I couldn't give a damn, frankly. It's you I'm thinking about, Donald, not me. I feel responsible for you, crazy as that sounds. I'm wondering whether I should let you go. You see, Donald, you're letting me get in the way of your work, aren't you?'

Maitland shrugged. 'In a sense, yes. What of it, though?'

Suddenly there was a slam of smashing glass and the French window burst open. A violent gust of wind ballooned the curtains back to the ceiling, knocking over a standard lamp and throwing a brilliant whirl of light along the walls. The force drove Maitland across the carpet. Outside there was the clatter and rattle of a score of dustbins, the banging of windows and doors. Maitland stepped forward, pushed back the curtains, and wrested the window shut. The wind leaned on it heavily, apparently coming from due east with almost gale force, bending the lower half of the frame clear of the hinges. He moved the sideboard across the doors, then set the standard lamp back on its base.

Susan was standing near the alcove by the bookcase, her face tense, anxiously fingering one of the empty glasses.

'It was like this at Worthing,' she said quietly. 'Some of the panes in the sun deck over the beach blew in and the wind just exploded. What do you think it means?'

'Nothing. It's the sort of freak weather you find in mid-Atlantic six months of the year.' He remembered the sun lounge over the beach, a bubble of glass panes that formed one end of the large twin-levelled room that was virtually the entire villa. 'You're lucky you weren't hit by flying glass. What did you do about the broken panes?'

Susan shrugged. 'We didn't do anything. That was the trouble. Two blew out, and then suddenly about ten more. Before we could move the wind was blowing straight through like a tornado.'

'What about Sylvester?' Maitland asked sardonically. 'Couldn't he pump up his broad shoulders and shield you from the tempest?'

'Donald, you don't understand.' Susan walked over to him. She seemed to have forgotten their previous dialogue. 'It was absolutely terrifying. It's not as bad up here in town, but along the coast – the seas are coming right over the

15

front, the beach road out to the villa isn't there any more. That's why we couldn't get anyone to come and help us. There are pieces of concrete the size of this room moving in and out on the tide. Peter had to get one of the farmers to tow us across the field with his tractor.'

Maitland looked at his watch. It was six o'clock, time for him to be on his way if he were to find a hotel for the night – though it looked as if most London hotels would be filled up.

'Strange,' he commented. He started to move for the door but Susan intercepted him, her face strained and flat, her long dark hair pushed back off her forehead, showing her narrow temple bones. 'Donald, please. Don't go yet. I'm worried about it. And there's all this dust.'

Maitland watched it settling towards the carpet, filtering through the yellow light like mist in a cloud chamber. 'I wouldn't worry, Susan,' he said. 'It'll blow over.' He gave her a weak smile and walked to the door. She followed him for a moment and then stopped, watching him silently. As he turned the handle he realized that he had already begun to forget her, his mind withdrawing all contact with hers, erasing all memories.

'See you some time,' he managed to say. Then he waved and stepped into the corridor, closing the door on a last glimpse of her stroking back her long hair, her eyes turning to the bar.

Collecting his suitcases from the service room on the floor above, he took the elevator down to the foyer and asked the porter to order a taxi. The streets outside were empty, the red dust lying thickly on the grass in the square, a foot deep against the walls at the far end. The trees switched and quivered under the impact of the wind, and small twigs and branches littered the roadway. While the taxi was coming he phoned London Airport, and after a long wait was told that all flights had been indefinitely suspended. Tickets were being refunded at booking offices and new bookings could only be made from a date to be announced later.

Maitland had changed all but a few pound notes into Canadian dollars. Rather than go to the trouble of changing it back again, he arranged to spend the next day or two until he could book a passage on one of the transatlantic liners with a close friend called Andrew Symington, an electronics engineer who worked for the Air Ministry.

Symington and his wife lived in a small house in Swiss Cottage. As the taxi made its way slowly through the traffic in Park Lane – the east wind had turned the side streets into corridors of high-pressure air that rammed against the stream of cars, forcing them down to a cautious fifteen or twenty miles an hour – Maitland pictured the sly ribbing the Symingtons would give him when they discovered that his long-expected departure for Canada had been abruptly postponed.

Andrew had warned him not to abandon his years of work at the Middlesex simply to escape from Susan and his sense of failure in having become involved with her. Maitland lay back in his seat, looking at the reflection of himself in the plate glass behind the driver, trying to decide how far Andrew had been right. Physiognomically he certainly appeared to be the exact opposite of the emotionally-motivated cycloid personality. Tall, and slightly stooped, his face was thin and firm, with steady eyes and a strong jaw. If anything he was probably over-resolute, too inflexible, a victim of his own rational temperament, viewing himself with the logic he applied in his own laboratory. How far this had made him happy was hard to decide. . . .

Horns sounded ahead of them and cars were slowing down in both traffic lanes. A moment later a brilliant catherine wheel of flickering light fell directly out of the air into the roadway in front of him.

Braking sharply, the driver pulled up without warning, and Maitland pitched forward against the glass pane, bruising his jaw viciously. As he stumbled back into the seat, face clasped in his hands, a vivid cascade of sparks played over the hood of the taxi. A line of power cables had come down in the wind and were arcing onto the vehicle, the gusts venting from one of the side streets tossing them into the air and then flinging them back onto the hood.

Panicking, the driver opened his door. Before he could steady himself the wind caught the door and wrenched it back, dragging him out onto the road. He stumbled to his feet by the front wheel, tripping over the long flaps of his overcoat. The sparking cables whipped down onto the hood and flailed across him like an enormous phosphorescent lash.

Still holding his face, Maitland leaped out of the cabin and jumped back onto the pavement, watching the cables flick backward and forward across the vehicle. The traffic had stopped, and a small crowd gathered among the stalled cars, watching at a safe distance as the thousands of sparks cataracted across the roadway and showered down over the twitching body of the driver.

An hour later, when he reached the Symingtons', the bruise on Maitland's jaw had completely stiffened the left side of his face. Soothing it with an icebag, he sat in an armchair in the lounge, sipping whisky and listening to the steady drumming of the wind on the wooden shutters across the windows.

'Poor devil. God knows if I'm supposed to attend the inquest. I should be on a boat within a couple of days.'

'Doubt if you will,' Symington said. 'There's nothing on the Atlantic at present. The *Queen Elizabeth* and the *United States* both turned back for New York today when they were only fifty miles out. This morning a big super-tanker

18

went down in the channel and we couldn't get a single rescue ship or plane to it.'

'How long has the wind kept up now?' Dora Symington asked. She was a plump, dark-haired girl, expecting her first baby.

'About a fortnight,' Symington said. He smiled warmly at his wife. 'Don't worry, though, it won't go on forever.'

'Well, I hope not,' his wife said. 'I can't even get out for a walk, Donald. And everything seems so dirty.'

'This dust, yes,' Maitland agreed. 'It's all rather curious.'

Symington nodded, watching the windows pensively. He was ten years older than Maitland, a small balding man with a wide round cranium and intelligent eyes.

When they had chatted together for about half an hour he helped his wife up to bed and then came down to Maitland, closing the doors and wedging them with pieces of felt.

'Dora's getting near her time,' he told Maitland. 'It's a pity all this excitement has come up.'

With Dora gone, Maitland realized how bare the room seemed, and noticed that all the Symingtons' glassware and ornaments, as well as an entire wall of books, had been packed away.

'You two moving house?' he asked, pointing to the empty shelves.

Symington shook his head. 'No, just taking a few precautions. Dora left the bedroom window slightly open this morning and a flying mirror damn near guillotined her. If the wind gets much stronger some really big things are going to start moving.'

Something about Symington's tone caught Maitland's attention.

'Do they expect it to get much stronger?' he asked.

'Well, as a matter of interest it's increasing by about five miles an hour each day. Of course it won't go on increasing indefinitely at that rate or we'll all be blown off the face of the earth – quite literally – but one can't be certain it'll begin to subside just when our particular patience has been exhausted.' He filled his glass with whisky, tipped in some water and then sat down facing Maitland, examining the bruise on his jaw. The dark swelling reached from his chin cleft up past the cheekbone to his temple.

Maitland nodded, listening to the rhythmic batter of the shutters above the steady drone of the wind. He realized that he had been too preoccupied with his abortive attempt to escape from England to more than notice the existence of the wind. At the airport he had regarded it as merely one facet of the weather, waiting, with the typical impatient optimism of every traveller, for it to die down and let him get on with the important business of boarding his aircraft.

'What do the weather experts think has caused it?' he asked.

'None of them seems to know. It certainly has some unusual features. I don't know whether you've noticed, but it doesn't let up, even momentarily.' He tilted his head towards the window behind him and Maitland listened to the steady unvarying whine passing through the maze of rooftops and chimneys.

He nodded to Symington. 'What's its speed now?'

'About fifty-five. Quite brisk, really. It's amazing that these old places can hold together even at that. I wouldn't like to be in Tokyo or Bangkok, though.'

Maitland looked up. 'Do you mean they're having the same trouble?'

Symington nodded. 'Same trouble, same wind. That's another curious thing about it. As far as we can make out, the wind force is increasing at the same rate all over the world. It's at its highest – about sixty miles an hour – at the equator, and diminishing gradually with latitude. In other words, it's almost as if a complete shell of solid air, with its axis at the poles, were revolving around the globe. There may be one or two minor variations where local prevailing winds overlay the global system, but its direction is constantly westward.' He looked at his watch. 'Let's catch the ten o'clock news. Should be on now.'

He switched on a portable radio, waited until the chimes had ended and then turned up the volume.

'... widespread havoc is reported from many parts of the world, particularly in the Far East and the Pacific, where tens of thousands are homeless. Winds of up to hurricane force have flattened entire towns and villages, causing heavy flooding and hampering the efforts of rescue workers. Our correspondent in New Delhi has stated that the Indian government is to introduce a number of relief measures. . . . For the fourth day in succession shipping has been at a standstill. . . . No news has yet been received of any survivors of the 65,000-ton tanker *Onassis Flyer*, which capsized in heavy seas in the channel early this morning. . . .'

Symington switched the set off, drummed his fingers lightly on the table. 'Hurricane is a slight exaggeration. A hundred miles an hour is a devastating speed. No relief work at all is possible; people are too busy trying to find a hole in the ground.'

Maitland closed his eyes, listened to the drumming of the shutters. Away in the distance somewhere a car horn sounded. London seemed massive and secure, a vast immovable citadel of brick and mortar compared with the flimsy bamboo cities of the Pacific seaboard.

Symington went off into his study, came back a few moments later with a rack of test tubes. He put it down on the table and Maitland sat forward to examine the tubes. There were half a dozen in all, neatly labelled and annotated. They each contained the same red-brown dust that Maitland had seen everywhere for the past few days. In the first tube there was a quarter of an inch, in the others progressively more, until the last tube held almost three inches.

Reading the labels, Maitland saw that they were dated.

'I've been measuring the daily dust fall,' Symington explained. 'There's a rain meter in the garden.'

Maitland held up the tube on the right. 'Nearly ten cc.s,' he remarked. 'Pretty heavy.' He raised the tube up to the light, shook the crystals from side to side. 'What are they? Looks almost like sand, but where the hell's it come from?'

Symington smiled sombrely. 'Not from the south coast, anyway. Quite a long way off. Out of curiosity I asked one of the soil chemists at the Ministry to analyse a sample. Apparently this is loess, the fine crystalline topsoil found in the alluvial plains of Tibet and Northern China. We haven't heard any news from there recently, and I'm not surprised. If the same concentrations of dust are falling all over the northern hemisphere, it means that something like fifty million tons of soil has been carted all the way across the Middle East and Europe and dumped on the British Isles alone, equal to the top two feet of our country's entire surface.'

Symington paced over to the window, then swung around on Maitland, his face tired and drawn. 'Donald, I have to admit it; I'm worried. Do you realize what the inertial drag is of such a mass? It should have stopped the wind in its tracks. God, if it can move the whole of Tibet without even a shrug, it can move anything.'

The telephone in the hall rang. Excusing himself, Symington stepped out of the lounge. He closed the door behind him without bothering to replace the strips of felt, and the constant pressure pulses caused by the wind striking the shutters finally jolted the door off its catch.

Through the narrow opening Maitland caught:

'. . . I thought we were supposed to be taking over the old RAF field at Tern Hill. The H-bomb bays there are over fifteen feet thick, and connected by underground bunkers. What? Well, tell the Minister that the minimum accomodation required for one person for a period longer than a month is three thousand cubic feet. If he crams thousands of people into those underground platforms they'll soon go mad –'

Symington came back and closed the door, then stared pensively at the floor.

'I'm afraid I couldn't help overhearing some of that,' Maitland said. 'Surely the goverment isn't taking emergency measures already?'

Symington eyed Maitland thoughtfully for a few seconds before he replied. 'No, not exactly. Just a few precautionary moves. There are people in the War Office whose job is to stay permanently three jumps ahead of the politicians. If the wind goes on increasing, say to hurricane force, there'll be a tremendous outcry in the House of Commons if we haven't prepared at least a handful of deep shelters. As long as one tenth of one per cent of the population are catered for, everybody's happy.' He paused bleakly for a moment. 'But God help the other 99.9.'

Windborne, the sound of engines murmured below the hill crest.

For a moment they echoed and reverberated in the airstream moving rapidly across the cold earth, then abruptly, 200 yards away, the horizon rose into the sky as the long lines of vehicles lumbered forward. Like gigantic robots assembling for some futuristic land battle, the vast graders and tournadozers, walking draglines and super-tractors edged slowly towards each other. They moved in two opposing lines, each composed of fifty vehicles, wheels as tall as houses, their broad tracks ten feet wide.

High above them, behind the hydraulic rams and metal grabs, their drivers sat almost motionless at their controls, swaying in their seats as the vehicles rolled through dips in the green turf. Clouds of exhaust poured from the vehicles' stacks, swept away by the dark wind, the throb of their engines filling the air with menacing thunder.

When the opposing lines were 200 yards from each other their flanks turned at right angles to form a huge square, and the entire assembly ground to a halt.

As the minutes passed only the wind could be heard, rolling and whining through the sharp metal angles of the machines. Then a small broad figure in a dark coat strode rapidly from the windward line of vehicles towards the centre of the arena. Here he paused, his head bared, revealing a massive domed forehead, small hard eyes and callous mouth. He turned his face to the wind, raising his head slightly, so that his heavy jaw pointed into it like the ironclad prow of an ancient dreadnought.

Surrounded by the long lines of machines, he stood looking beyond them, the wind dragging at the flaps of his coat, his eyes questing through the low storm clouds that fled past as if trying to escape his gaze.

Glancing at his watch, he raised his arm, clenched his fist above his head and then dropped it sharply.

With a roar of racing clutches and exhausts, the huge

vehicles snapped into motion. Tracks skating in the soft earth, wheels spinning, they plunged and jostled, the long lines breaking into a mass of slamming metal.

As they moved away to their tasks the iron-faced man stood silently, ignoring them, his eyes still searching the wind.

Chapter 2

From the Submarine Pens

FROM: ADMIRAL HAMILTON, CIC US SIXTH FLEET, USS EISENHOWER, TUNIS. TO COMMANDER LANYON, USS TERRAPIN, GENOA: GENERAL VAN DAMM NOW IN US MILITARY HOSPITAL, NICE. MULTIPLE SPINAL FRACTURES. COLLECT TROOP CARRIER FROM NATO TRANSPORT POOL, GENOA. EXPECTED WIND SPEED: 85 KNOTS.

Crouched down in the well of the conning tower, Lanyon scanned the message, then nodded to the sailor, who saluted and disappeared below.

Twenty feet above him the concrete roof of the submarine pen was slick with moisture which dripped steadily into the choppy water below. The steel gates of the pen had been closed, but the sea outside pounded against the heavy grilles. It drove high swells along the 300-foot length of the pen which rode the *Terrapin* up and down on its moorings and then slapped against the far wall, sending clouds of spray into the air over the submarine's stern.

Lanyon waited until the last of the moorings had been completed, then waved briefly to the portmaster, a blond-haired lieutenant in the concrete control cage jutting out from the wall ten feet ahead. Lowering himself through the hatch, he climbed down the companionway into the control room, swung around the periscope well and made his way to his cabin.

He sat down on his bunk and slowly loosened his collar, adjusting himself to the rhythmic rise and fall of the submarine. After the three-day crossing of the Mediterranean, at a steady, comfortable twenty fathoms, the surface felt like a switchback. His instructions were to make one trial surfacing en route, in a sheltered cove off the west coast of Sicily. But even before the conning tower broke surface the *Terrapin* took on a 30-degree yaw and was hit by tremendous seas that almost stood it on its stern. They had stayed down until reaching the comparatively sheltered waters of the submarine base at Genoa, but even there had a difficult job negotiating the wreck-strewn limbs of the double breakwater.

What it was like topside Lanyon hated to imagine. Tunis, where all that was left of the Sixth Fleet was bottled up, had been a complete shambles. Vast seas were breaking over the harbour area, sending two-foot waves down streets 300 yards inshore, slamming at the big 95,000-ton carrier *Eisenhower* and the two cruisers moored against the piers. When he had last seen the *Eisenhower* she had taken on a twenty-five-degree list and the constant fifty-foot rise and fall had begun to rip huge pieces of concrete from the sides of the pier.

Genoa, sheltered a little by the hills and the land mass of the peninsula, seemed to be quieter. With luck, Lanyon hoped, the military here would have their pants on, instead of running around like a lot of startled baboons, frightening themselves with their own noise.

Lanyon tossed his cap onto the desk and stretched out on the bunk. As a submariner he felt (irrationally, he knew) that the wind was everybody else's problem. At thirty-eight he had served in submarines for over fifteen years, ever since he left Annapolis, and the traditional self-sufficiency of the service was now part of him. A sparse, lean six-footer, to strangers he appeared withdrawn and moody, but he had long ago found that a detached viewpoint left him with more freedom to manoeuvre.

So Van Damm was still alive. The captain who had laid on the *Terrapin* had told Lanyon confidentially that the general would almost certainly be dead by the time they reached Genoa, but whether this was the truth or merely an astute piece of psychology – everybody else in the crew seemed to have been fed the same story – Lanyon had no means of finding out. Certainly Van Damm had been severely injured in the plane smash at Orly Airport, but at least he was lucky enough to be alive. The five-man crew of the Constellation and two of the general's aides had been killed outright.

Now Van Damm had been brought south to Nice and the *Terrapin* would have another shot at rescuing him. Lanyon wondered whether it was worth it. Up to the time of his accident Van Damm had been expected to declare himself the Democratic candidate in the coming election, but he wouldn't be of much interest now to the party chiefs. However, presumably some debt of honour was being paid off. After three years as NATO Supreme Commander, Van Damm was due anyway for retirement, and probably the Pentagon was living up to its bargain with him when he had signed on.

There was a knock on the door and Lieutenant Matheson, Lanyon's number two, stuck his head in.

'O.K., Steve?'

Lanyon swung his legs off the bunk. 'Sure, come in.'

Matheson looked slightly anxious, his plump face tense and uneven.

'I hear Van Damm is still holding on? Thought he was supposed to peg out by now.'

Lanyon shrugged. The *Terrapin* was a small J-class sub, and apart from himself Matheson was the only officer aboard. What frightened him was that he might have to take on the job of driving up to Nice and collecting Van Damm.

Lanyon smiled to himself. He liked Matheson, a pleasant boy with a relaxed sense of humour that Lanyon appreciated. But Matheson was no hero.

'What's the programme now?' Matheson pressed. 'It's

a 250-mile run round the coast to Nice, and God knows what it might be like. Don't you think it's worth trying to get in a little closer? There's a deep anchorage at Monte¯ Carlo.'

Lanyon shook his head. 'It's full of smashed-up yachts. I can't take the risk. Don't worry, wind speed's only about ninety. It'll probably start slacking off today.'

Matheson snorted unhappily. 'That's what they've been saying for the last three weeks. I think we'd be crazy to lose two or three men trying to rescue a stiff.'

Lanyon let this pass, but in a quiet voice he said: 'Van Damm isn't dead yet. He's done his job, so I think we ought to do ours.'

He stood up and pulled a heavy leather windbreaker from a hook on the bulkhead over the desk, then buckled on a service .45 and glanced at himself in the mirror, straightening his uniform.

After putting on his cap, he opened the door. 'Let's go and see what's happening on deck.'

They made their way up to the conning tower, crossed the gangway onto the narrow jetty on the wall of the sub-pen. A stairway took them over the workshops into the control deck at the far end of the pens.

There were a dozen pens in all, each with room for four submarines, but only three ships were at their berths, fitting out for rescue missions similar to the *Terrapin*'s.

All the windows they passed were bricked in, but even through three feet of concrete they could hear the steady unvarying drone of the storm wind.

A sailor guided them to one of the offices in Combined Personnel H.Q. where Major Hendrix, the liaison officer, greeted them and pulled up chairs.

The office was snug and comfortable, but something about Hendrix, the fatigue showing in his face, the two buttons missing from his uniform jacket, warned Lanyon that he could expect to find conditions less equable outside.

'Good to see you, Commander,' Hendrix said hurriedly. A couple of map wallets and a packet of currency were on his desk and he pushed them forward. 'Forgive me if I come straight to the point, but the army is pulling out of Genoa today and I've got a million things to do.' He glanced up at the wall clock for a moment, then flipped on the intercom. 'Sergeant, what are the latest readings we've got?'

'A hundred fifteen and 265 degrees magnetic, sir.'

Hendrix looked up at Lanyon. 'A hundred fifteen miles an hour and virtually due east, Commander. The troop carrier is waiting for you out in the transport bay. There are a navy driver and a couple of orderlies from the sick bay here.' He stood up and moved around his desk. 'The coast road is still open, apparently, but watch out for collapsing buildings through the towns.' He looked at Matheson. 'I take it the lieutenant will be going to pick up Van Damm, Commander.'

Lanyon shook his head. 'No, as a matter of fact I will be, Captain.'

'Wait a minute, sir,' Matheson started to cut in, but Lanyon waved him back.

'It's O.K., Paul. I'd like to have a look at the scenery.'

Matheson made a further token protest, then said no more.

They made their way out to the transport bay, the sounds of the wind growing steadily louder as they passed down the corridors. Revolving doors had been built into the exits, each operated by a couple of men with powerful winches.

They picked up the driver and Lanyon turned to Matheson. 'I'll call you in six hours' time, when we make the border. Check with Hendrix here and let me know if anything comes in from Tunis.'

Zipping his jacket, he nodded to the driver and stepped through into the entry section of the door. The men on the winch cranked it around and Lanyon stepped out into sharp daylight and a vicious tornado of air that whirled past him, jockeying him across a narrow yard between two high concrete buildings. Stinging clouds of grit and sand sang through the air, lashing at his face and legs. Before he could grab it, his peaked cap sailed up into the air and shot away on a tremendous updraught.

Holding tight to the map wallets, he lurched across to the troop carrier, a squat twelve-wheeler with sandbags strapped to the hood and over the windshield, and heavy steel shutters welded to the window grilles.

Inside, two orderlies squatted down silently on a mattress. They were wearing one-piece plastic suits fitted with hoods roped tightly around their faces, so that only their eyes and mouths showed. Bulky goggles hung from their necks. Lanyon climbed over into the co-driver's seat and waited for the driver to bolt up the doors. It was dim and cold inside the carrier, the sole light coming from the wide periscope mirror mounted over the dashbord. The doors and control pedals were taped with cotton wadding, but a steady stream of air whistled through the clutch and brake housings, chilling Lanyon's legs.

He peered through the periscope. Directly ahead, straight into the wind, he could see down a narrow asphalt roadway past a line of high buildings, the rear walls of the sub-pens. A quarter of a mile away was what looked like the remains of a boundary fence, tilting posts from which straggled a few strands of barbed wire. Beyond the boundary was a thick grey haze, blurred and shimmering, a tremendous surface dust-storm two or three hundred feet high, which headed straight towards them and then passed overhead. Looking up, he saw that it contained thousands of miscellaneous objects – bits of paper and refuse, rooftiles, leaves, and fragments of glass – all borne aloft on a huge sweeping tide of dust.

The driver took his seat, switched on the radio and spoke

to Traffic Control. Receiving his clearance, he gunned the engine and edged forward into the wind.

The carrier ground along at a steady ten miles an hour, passed the sub-pens and then turned along the boundary road. As it pivoted, the whole vehicle tilted sideways, caught and held by the tremendous power of the wind. No longer shielded by the sandbags, there was a continuous clatter and rattle as scores of hard objects bounced off the sloping sides of the carrier, each report as loud as a ricocheting bullet.

'Feels like a space ship going through a meteor shower,' Lanyon commented.

The driver, a tough young Brooklyner called Goldman, nodded. 'Yeah, there's some really big stuff moving now, Commander.'

Lanyon looked out through the periscope. This had a 90-degree traverse and afforded a satisfactorily wide sweep of the road ahead. A quarter of a mile away were the gates into the base and a cluster of single-storey guard houses, half obscured by the low-lying dust cloud. On the right were big two- and three-storey blocks, fuel depots, with their underground tanks, windows sand-bagged, exposed service plant swathed in canvas.

Genoa lay behind them to the south, hidden in the haze. They swung out through the gateway and took the coast road that ran about half a mile inland, a wide concrete motorway cut into the leeward side of the low hills reaching towards the mountain shield at Alassio. All the crops in the adjacent fields had long been flattened, but the heavy stone farmhouses nestling in saddles between the hills were still intact, their roofs weighed down with tiers of flagstones.

They passed through a succession of drab villages, windows boarded up against the storm, alleyways jammed with the wrecks of old cars and farm implements. In the main square of Larghetto a bus lay on its side, and headless statues stood over the empty fountains. The roof of the fourteenth-century town hall had gone, but most of the buildings and houses they saw, despite their superficially decrepit appearance, were well able to withstand the hurrican-force winds. They were probably stronger than the mass-produced modern split-levels and ranch homes of the big housing developments back in the States.

'Can you pick up any news on this rig?' Lanyon asked Goldman, pointing to the radio.

The driver switched on and swung the dials, avoiding the army and navy channels.

'For once the air force got nothing to say,' he commented with a short laugh. 'AFN Munich should still be on the air.'

A rain of pebbles against the side of the carrier drowned out a newcaster's voice, but turning up the volume Lanyon heard:

'. . . no news available on the Pacific area, but heavy flooding and winds of hurricane force are believed to have caused thousands of casualties in islands as far apart as Okinawa and the Solomons. Indian Prime Minister Pandit Nehru has outlined full-scale relief measures, and Iraq and Persia are to collaborate in organizing essential supplies to stricken towns and villages. In the UN Assembly the Afro-Asian bloc has tabled a resolution calling on the United Nations to launch a global relief mission. Widespread flooding has brought unprecedented damage to the Middle West. Damage is estimated at four hundred million dollars, but so far few lives have been taken. . . .'

That's one good thing, Lanyon thought. The flooding might bring the danger of typhoid and cholera, but so far, at least, even in the Pacific area, loss of life had been low. A hurricane like the one he had seen down at the base at Key West two years earlier had swooped in from the Caribbean without any warning, and just about the whole Atlantic seaboard had caught without warning. Scores of people had been killed driving their cars home. This time, though, the gradual build-up in speed, the steady five miles an hour

33

daily increase, had given everyone a chance to nail the roof down, dig a deep shelter in the garden or basement, lay in food stocks.

They passed through San Remo, the lines of hotels shuddering as the wind thrashed across the hundreds of shuttered balconies. Below, the sea writhed and flickered with mountainous waves, and spray dropped the visibility down to little more than a mile.

One or two vehicles passed them, crawling along under loads of sandbags. Most of them were Italian military or police trucks, patrolling the windswept empty streets.

Lanyon dozed off in the cold greasy air inside the carrier. He woke just as they crossed the main square of a small town and heard a heavy pounding on the steel plates behind his head.

The blows repeated themselves at rapid intervals, and through the thick armour plating Lanyon heard the dim sounds of someone shouting.

He sat up and peered into the periscope, but the cobbled street ahead was empty.

'What's going on?' he asked the driver.

Goldman flipped away the butt of his cigarette. 'Some sort of rumpus back there, Commander. Couldn't make it out exactly.'

He leaned a little harder on the accelerator, pushed the carrier's speed up to fifteen miles an hour. The pounding stopped, then took up again more insistently, the voice hoarser above the wind.

Lanyon tapped the steering wheel. 'Slow down for a second. I'll go back and check.'

Goldman started to protest, but Lanyon straddled the back of his seat, stepped past the two orderlies sitting on the mattress, and got to the rear doors. He slipped back the shutters, peered out through the grille. A small group of people clustered around the porch of a grey-walled church on the north side of the square. There were several women among them, all wearing black shawls over their heads, backing into the recessed entranceway. A loose heap of rubble lay in the square at their feet and clouds of dust and mortar were falling around them.

The church tower was missing. A single spur of brickwork, all that was left of one corner, stood up fifteen feet above the apex of the roof. The wind was tearing at the raw masonry, stripping away whole pieces of brick.

One of the orderlies crawled across the mattress and crouched next to Lanyon.

'The tower's just collapsed,' Lanyon told him. He indicated the stack of cartons. 'What have you got inside there?'

'Plasma, oxygen, pencillin.' The orderly peered at Lanyon. 'We can't use it on them, Commander. This stuff's reserved for the general.'

'Don't worry, they'll have more supplies at Nice.'

'But Commander, they may have run out. Casualties are probably pouring in there. It's a small hospital – just a dysentery unit for overtired weekenders on the Paris mill.'

Just then a figure appeared around the end of the carrier and pressed his face to the grille, jabbering in Italian. It was a big gaunt man with bulky shoulders, and black hair low over a tough face.

The orderly backed away but Lanyon started to open the doors. Over his shoulder he shouted at Goldman.

'Reverse up towards the church! I'll see if we can lend a hand.'

'Commander, once we start helping these people we'll never get to Nice. They've got their own rescue units working.'

'Not right here, anyway. Come on, you heard me, back in!'

As he slipped the catch the big Italian outside wrenched the door out of his hands. He looked angry and exhausted, and pulled Lanyon out of the truck, yelling at him and pointing at the church. Goldman was reversing the carrier out of the street into the square, the orderlies jumping down and bolting the door behind them.

As they reached the church, brickwork and plaster shattered down onto the pavement around them. The Italian shouldered his way through the people in the entranceway, and led Lanyon through into the nave.

Inside the church, a bomb appeared to have exploded in the middle of a crowded congregation. A group of women and older men and children crouched around the altar while the priest and five or six younger men pulled away the mounds of masonry that had fallen through the roof when the tower had collapsed, taking with it one of the longitudinal support beams. This lay across the pews. Below it, through the piles of white dust and masonry, Lanyon could see tags of black fabric, twisted shoes, the hunched forms of crouching bodies.

Above them, the wind racing across the surface of the roof was stripping away the ragged edge of tiles around the ten-foot-wide hole, hampering the men tearing away the rubble over the pews. Lanyon joined the big Italian at one end of the roof beam, but they failed to move it.

Lanyon turned to leave the nave and the big Italian ran after him and seized his shoulder, his face contorted with anger and fatigue.

'Not go!' he bellowed. He pointed to the pile of rubble. 'My wife, my wife! You stay!'

Lanyon tried to pacify him, indicated the truck that had backed into the entranceway, its doors open, one of the orderlies crouched inside. He tore himself from the Italian and ran out to the truck, shouting: 'Goldman, get the winch running. Where's the cable?'

They pulled it out of the locker under the end board, clipped it into the winch and then carried the free end through into the nave. Lanyon and the Italian lashed it to the main beam, then Goldman gunned up the great 550 hp engine and tautened the cable, slowly swinging the beam sideways off the pew into the centre of the aisle. Immediately two or three people trapped below the pews began to stir. One of them, a young woman wearing the remains of a black dress that was now as white as a bridal gown, managed to stand up weakly and pulled herself out. Between her feet Lanyon could see several motionless figures, and the big Italian was digging frantically with his hands at the masonry, hurling it away with insane force.

More figures pressed into the nave behind him, and Lanyon turned to see that a squad of uniformed troops, with a couple of police carabinieri, had arrived, carrying in stretchers and plasma kits.

'Every thanks, Captain,' the sergeant told him. 'We are all grateful to your men.' He shook his head sadly, glancing around at the church. 'The people were praying for the stop of the wind.'

Lanyon and the orderlies climbed back into the carrier, sealed the doors and moved off.

Massaging his bruised hands and trying to regain his breath, Lanyon turned to the orderlies slumped down on the mattress. 'Did either of you see whether that big fellow got his wife out?'

They shook their heads doubtfully. 'Don't think so, Commander.'

Goldman accelerated the engine and straightened the periscope. 'Wind speed's up, Commander. One ten now. We'll have to keep moving if we're going to make Nice by dark.'

Lanyon studied the driver for a few moments, watching the cigarette butt rotate nastily around his mouth. 'Don't worry, sailor,' he said, 'I'll concentrate on the general from now on.'

They crossed the border at Vintemille at 7 p.m. and cleared through by radio with Nice and Genoa. The flimsy customs sheds and wooden turnpikes had disappeared; the frontier guards on both sides were dug into sandbagged emplacements below ground surface.

They reached Nice within a couple of hours, taking the Corniche road through the hills. The hospital compound was packed with hundreds of trucks and jeeps, their drivers huddled in the entrances to the loading bays. A couple of MPs steered the carrier over to one of the rear wings, where Lanyon and the orderlies climbed out and battled their way inside.

'You're later than expected, Commander,' a burly red-faced major in reception greeted Lanyon. 'I gather it's really blowing up outside.'

He led Lanyon into a side office where there were coffee and hot rolls on a table.

Lanyon pulled off his leather jacket and helped himself to coffee, then sat down thankfully on a teak chest resting on a low table against the wall.

Putting out his cigarette, the major hurriedly pushed across a canvas chair.

'Sorry, Commander, but perhaps you'd better sit on this. Don't want to show any disrespect to the general, do we?'

Lanyon pulled himself to his feet. 'What are you talking about?' he asked, puzzled. 'Which general?'

The major smiled. 'Van Damm.' He pointed to the teak box. 'You were sitting on him.'

Lanyon put down his coffee. 'Do you mean that Van Damm's dead?' When the major nodded he stared down at the coffin, shaking his head slowly. It was ringed with heavy steel tape, and there was a Graves Commission seal franked with a Paris movement order.

The major began to laugh noiselessly to himself, looking Lanyon's wind-torn uniform up and down and shaking his head in dry amusement. Lanyon waited for him to finish.

'Now tell me what's really inside,' he asked. 'An atom bomb, or somebody's favourite spaniel?'

Still chuckling, the major took out a silver hip flask, plucked a paper cup from the water dispenser in the corner and passed them across the table to Lanyon.

'No, it's Van Damm all right. It may seem a hell of a time to take him home, but he's booked into Arlington Cemetery and if he doesn't go now there's a good chance he never will. There just won't be room.'

Lanyon helped himself to a shot of whisky. 'So he *was* dead after the crash?'

'He was dead *before* the crash. Van Damm was killed two weeks ago in a car smash in Spain. He was on some private visit to Franco, which they had hushed up for political reasons, in case it hurt his campaign. His body was being shipped home on the plane. Nobody survived the crack-up at Orly. The Connie went straight into the deck on her back before she made 300 feet. Flipped right over like a paper dart. They fished out Van Damm's bits and pieces and decided to mail 'em collect to Nice.' He replaced the flask, then went over to the coffin and patted it gently. 'Well, have a quiet trip back to the States, General. You're the only one who will.'

Lanyon spent the night at the Hotel Europe, a big three-storey pile about five blocks back from the beach. The high clustering buildings in the hotel district made the streets just negotiable. Most of the hoteliers, with the aid of local shopkeepers, had built narrow roofed corridors of sandbags against the walls of the streets, and a maze of these dingy tunnels criss-crossed the city. A good number of bars and bistros were still open, and at the Hotel Europe forty or fifty people sat up most of the night in the bar, listening to the news reports and speculating about possible escape routes.

Lanyon gathered that the wind showed no signs yet

of abating; its rate of increase was still a steady five mph a day, by the latest estimates 117. After the initial period of inaction at last some organized attempt to preserve order was being made. Governments were requisitioning coal mines and deep shelters, stockpiling food and medical supplies. News reports were conflicting, but apparently most of Europe and American were still little more than inconvenienced, while South America, Africa and the East had suffered complete dislocation, and the first signs of famine and epidemic were revealing themselves.

They set off back for Genoa at seven the next morning, the teak coffin, sealed into a canvas shroud, stowed in the cabin under the mattress. Goldman had mouthed some bitter cynicism and he obviously regarded Lanyon as the representative of the worst perfidies of the officer caste. Lanyon himself felt mildly disgusted with Hamilton for wasting the *Terrapin's* potential, but the admiral might himself have been ignorant of Van Damm's death.

Five miles from Monte Carlo they passed through a small village, nestling below a cliff topped by big white hotels. The road narrowed, high walls on either side, and suddenly Goldman swore and braked the carrier. Lanyon peered into the periscope and saw two windswept figures in oilskins standing in the centre of the roadway, waving their arms in wide circles. When they neared the people Lanyon noticed a stack of pastel suitcases on the pavement, the gaudy airline stickers clearly visible.

'Hold it,' Lanyon snapped at Goldman. 'They're Americans. Must have been stranded here.'

They stopped the carrier and the orderlies unbolted the rear doors. Leaning out, Lanyon waved the two figures over, caught a glimpse of faces at the window of a house behind them.

One of the men climbed up onto the tail board and sat panting in long painful gasps.

'Thanks a million for stopping,' he said, touching Lanyon's shoulders gratefully. 'We'd just about given up.' He was about forty-five, a slimly-built man with greying hair and small neat features.

'How many of you are there?' Lanyon asked, pulling the door shut to shield them from the savage gusts that drove into the carrier and swept out every vestige of warmth.

'Just four. My name's Charlesby, US consul at Menton. There's Wilson, my deputy, his wife, and a girl from NBC. We were supposed to be covering the evacuation of American nationals to Paris, but everything's gone to hell. Our car cracked up, and we've been stuck here for a couple of days.'

The other man in oilskins ran across the road to the carrier, shielding a red-haired woman in white raincoat and plastic bootees. They pulled her up into the carrier, helped her back onto the mattress. Lanyon and the orderly jumped down into the road and ran over to the suit-cases, just as the other woman, wearing a tightly-belted blue coat, her blonde hair swirling around her head, ran out of the house and stepped nimbly across the pavement in long strides to the carrier. She tried to pick up one of the suitcases, but Lanyon pulled it from her hands, put his arm around her shoulders and steered her over to the open doors.

As the carrier got under way again Lanyon climbed forward and squatted down behind his seat. The two women were sitting back on the mattress, while Charlesby and Wilson crouched among the suitcases.

'We're making for Genoa,' Lanyon told Charlesby. 'Where are you people supposed to be heading for?'

Charlesby unbuttoned his oilskin.

'Paris, theoretically, or in an emergency the air force base near Toulon. I take it this rates as an emergency, but how that gets us to Toulon I haven't worked out yet.'

'I'd take you back to the hospital at Nice,' Lanyon said,

'but we can't spare the time. I'm afraid you'll have to ride back to Genoa with us and then see if you can pick up something going the other way.' He watched Wilson, a young man of about twenty-five, warming the chapped hands of his wife, a pale tired-looking girl who looked a few years younger. 'O.K., there?' Lanyon asked. When Wilson nodded, he turned to the girl in the blue coat sitting on the mattress beside him.

'What about you? Genoa suit you?'

'Uh-huh. Thanks a lot, Commander.' She pinned back her hair, looking Lanyon up and down. Her face was strong and full-lipped, with wide intelligent eyes that examined the commander with frank interest.

'Charlesby said you were with NBC. News reporter?'

She nodded, took a cigarette from the pack Lanyon offered her. As the carrier swung around a corner she rolled slightly against him, and Lanyon felt warm strong shoulders through her tightly-fitting coat.

She steadied herself with one hand on his arm, blew out a long straight stream of blue smoke.

'Patricia Olsen,' she introduced herself. 'On the Paris bureau. Came down here last week to get some shots for the folks back home of Monte Carlo being flattened.' She tapped the tape recorder next to her with one finger. 'All I've managed to get on this thing is the sound of my own screaming.'

Lanyon laughed and climbed into his seat. The carrier slowed down to a crawl and Goldman stabbed a finger at the periscope. They were moving straight into the wind, up a long narrow slope. Twenty yards ahead of them, caught by its bumpers between the walls of two houses, was a long black Buick, swung up onto one side by the force of the wind. Slowly it worked itself free, then rolled onto its back and slithered down the street towards them. Goldman accelerated sharply, and the Buick locked for a moment against the heavy nose armour, then lifted sharply into the air and careened over the sandbagged hood with a tremendous clatter, rolling off the roof of the carrier. For a moment the periscope was darkened. Then it cleared and they all turned to watch through the rear-door grilles as the Buick, its body holed and dented, slithered down the street, demolishing a low wall, from which clouds of dust took off in the air like supercharged steam.

'Bad driver,' Patricia Olsen commented dryly.

They quieted, listening to the holocaust hammering past outside. They were travelling due east, straight into the wind face, and the turbulence around the rear doors exploded periodically with sharp pressure booms. The streets outside thudded with the sounds of falling masonry, the eerie piercing scream of tinplate and galvanized iron being stripped from rooftops, the explosive shatter of snapping glass.

For hours they sat bunched together silently, swaying in unison with the motion of the carrier, trying to massage a little warmth into themselves.

'How long do you think most of the buildings can stand up to this wind?' Patricia Olsen asked Lanyon quietly.

Lanyon shrugged. 'If they're well built, they're probably O.K. up to about 150 mph. After that it looks as if we'll really have to hold onto our hats. How are you getting back to Paris? Most heavy transport has been requisitioned by the military.'

'I don't know whether I want to get back to Paris. Too many old chimneypots there.'

Lanyon glanced at his watch. It was 4.05. They had crossed the border and with luck would make Genoa in a couple of hours. Soon he'd be safely inside the *Terrapin* and away from this madness. Oddly, though, however little he ultimately cared about the people hiding in basements in the towns through which they had passed, he found himself wondering what would happen to the girl next to him. He

43

listened to the strong low sounds of her breathing; she looked highly adaptable and resourceful.

'Commander' Goldman shouted, almost standing up at the wheel, his eyes fixed on the periscope. They were about ten miles from Genoa, moving down an exposed section of road that curved towards the dam at Sestra, two miles away. The broad hump of the concrete barrier was obscured by the spray whipped up from the deep torrent of water swirling down the road fifty yards away from them. Just ahead it left the roadway and spilled down into the valley, carrying with it a foam-flecked jetsam of smashed sheds and chicken coops.

'The dam's gone, Commander!' Goldman bellowed. Frantically he reversed the engine, sent the carrier backing obliquely across the road. Lanyon pressed his eyes to the periscope, then wrenched at Goldman's shoulder. High waves were cascading down into the valley, but as far as he could see the dam's outline was intact.

'Goldman, snap out of it! The dam's still O.K.!' He pounded Goldman's shoulder. 'Get the engine forward again! The water's only a couple of feet deep.'

Carried by the wind, the carrier was reversing rapidly. Before Goldman could pull himself together the off-side rear wheels left the road, and the vehicle swung around sharply and rolled over onto its side.

With a savage jolt the occupants were hurled off balance against the roof. Lanyon pulled himself away from Goldman, struggled painfully through the dim light past Patricia Olsen, who was rubbing her knees. Charlesby and the Wilsons were getting to their feet among the mêlée of suitcases and medical cartons. One of the orderlies opened the doors and kicked them outward. A whirl of dust and gravel whipped off the surface of the road and flashed past them in a white blur, while ten yards away to their left a deep stream of icy water surged past down the valley, spreading out across the vineyards.

The carrier lay immovably on its side, wheels spinning in the wind. Lanyon looked around for Goldman, trying to decide whether to clap the man under arrest, then decided the gesture would prove nothing.

Half a mile away was a group of low two-storey brick buildings, grouped in a loose rectangle, a concrete tower standing above them on the far side. The remains of a rough fence ringed the compound, and there appeared to be a motor pool between two of the buildings, a collection of trucks huddled together against the storm.

'Looks like a barracks,' Lanyon decided. The intervening country consisted of narrow farm strips divided by heavy hedges, ten-foot-high bocage that would provide them with enough shelter to reach the buildings.

Charlesby wearily pulled himself over to the doorway. 'There's a good chance nothing will come along here for hours,' Lanyon told him. 'The road over the dam is probably closed by now and my guess is that they'll have radioed across to the units on this side to take another route further inland. We could be stranded here for days.' He pointed to the buildings in the distance. 'Just about our only hope is to head for the barracks over there.'

Lanyon leading, followed by Charlesby and the Wilsons, with Patricia Olsen and then Goldman and the two orderlies bringing up the rear, they dived out of the carrier and plunged down the slope towards the hedge running parallel to the road fifty yards away.

As he left the carrier the wind caught Lanyon and gunned him along, tossing him helplessly across the lumpy soil. Over his shoulder he caught a glimpse of the others stepping tentatively out of the carrier and being whirled away on the slipstream. Charlesby stumbled and fell onto his knees, and then was swept upright again, his legs racing madly. The Wilsons, arm in arm, were being buffeted from left to right like drunken circus clowns. Abruptly Lanyon lost his own footing, fell heavily onto his knees and was tossed sideways like a child rolling down a hill.

Regaining his balance, he reached the hedge, crawled along to a narrow gateway and slipped through it into the slightly sheltered lee of the hedge. Away in the distance Goldman was bowed down with his back to the wind, being carried along the verge of the roadway. Charlesby, oilskin ripped off his back and billowing over his head, only attached by the tapes under his armpits, followed ten yards behind.

Zigzagging along the hedges in the general direction of the barracks, Lanyon kept what lookout he could for the others. Once or twice he thought he saw one of them moving along an adjacent field, but he was unable to cross the intervening open ground.

He reached the boundary of the barracks within half an hour, and lay in a ditch on the inner side of the fence – nothing more now than a series of tilting support posts – scanning the open surface of the compound. The barracks was the airmen's quarters of a small airfield. Beyond the buildings were the control tower and two or three wide concrete runways extending off into the haze. Between the barracks he could see the upright steel skeletons of two large hangars. In the nearer hangar was the tail section of a Dakota that had been tethered by a steel hawser. It slammed and swivelled in the driving wind, its identification numerals still visible.

He was lying waiting in the ditch for any of the others to appear, when he noticed something rolling towards the boundary line about fifty yards away. It moved in sudden jerks, occasionally throwing up a narrow white limb that Lanyon recognized as an arm. Within a few seconds it reached the boundary line, crossed it and then rolled down into the ditch, a lumpy bundle of grey-and-black rags. Lanyon crawled along to it.

When he was a few feet away he recognized the tattered strips of Charlesby's oilskin, the shreds of his grey suit.

He reached Charlesby and straightened him out, then massaged his pallid face, heavily bruised and barely recognizable after being dragged across the rough farmland. For a few fruitless moments Lanyon pumped the man's lungs, trying to inject some movement into him. Finally he gave up, wrapped Charlesby's head in the skirt of the oilskin, and lashed it around his neck with his trouser belt. Soon the wind would let up and all the field rats and scavengers sheltering in their burrows would come out, searching a barren world for food. It might be some while before the body was found, and better the scavengers should start on Charlesby's hands than on his face.

As he backed away he saw someone approaching him along the ditch.

'Commander Lanyon!'

It was Patricia Olsen. She still wore the belted blue coat, scratched and muddied, and her blonde hair trailed around her head in a tangled mat.

He hurried along to her, took her arm and steadied her into a sitting position. She rolled her head weakly against his shoulder and glanced at the body.

'Charlesby?' When Lanyon nodded, she closed her eyes. 'Poor devil. Where are the others?'

'You're the only one I've seen.' Lanyon peered up at the sky. He felt exhausted and muscle weary, and he was sure that the wind was stronger than when they left the carrier an hour earlier. The air was full of large pieces of grit that flicked and stung at their faces like angry insects.

'We'd better get inside the barracks. Are you strong enough to make it?'

She nodded weakly. After a moment's rest they darted forward across the clipped turf to the building fifty yards away. Lanyon held her arm, and she was almost flung out of his grasp, but together they lurched over to the far end of the barracks and pulled themselves around the corner into the doorway.

At the rear of the entrance hall a stairway led below into the basement. They hurried down, tripping over the litter-strewn steps, and with luck found a more or less airtight room off the central corridor.

Patricia sat down weakly on an old bedstead and brushed her hair wearily off her face, drawing her coat over her long legs. Lanyon checked the window. Below ground level, it looked out onto the narrow well which ringed the building, but its shutters still held, though enough light filtered through for him to see around the room. There were a couple of bunks, two empty wall cupboards, and underfoot a collection of old movie magazines, discarded webbing and cigarette butts. Lanyon sat down on the bed next to her.

'Pat, I'm going upstairs in case there's anyone else here. May even be a telephone line still working.'

She nodded, curling up into the corner. She looked almost dead and Lanyon wondered whether the Wilsons had survived.

The barracks was empty. Upstairs, the wind raced through the broken windows like a tornado, ripping the cupboards from the walls and piling the bedsteads into tangled heaps. He found an internal phone in one of the offices, but the line was dead. The station had obviously been abandoned days earlier.

'Any luck?' Pat asked when he went down to the basement.

He shook his head. 'Looks as if we're stuck here. There are some wrecked trucks in a bay on the other side of the parade square. If the wind dies down a little tomorrow I may be able to salvage something that'll get us to Genoa.'

'Do you think it *will* die down?'

'Everybody keeps asking me that.' Lanyon hung his head for a moment. 'It's curious, but until I saw Charlesby lying in that ditch I didn't feel all that concerned. In a way I was almost glad. So much of life in the States – and over here for that matter – could use a strong breath of fresh air. But I realize now that a garbage-disposal job of this size rakes away too much of the good along with the bad.'

He grinned at her suddenly. She smiled back, eyeing him with a long steady gaze, one he felt no hesitation in returning. With her blue coat and clear white skin against the drab background of the basement wall, she reminded him of the madonna in the gilt frame over the altarpiece in the wrecked church. The woman's hair had been black, but her robes had glowed with the same luminescent quality as Pat's ash-blonde hair.

Outside, the wind hurled itself across the dark swell of the land.

The hill had gone, obliterated beneath the gigantic jaws of the fleets of bulldozers, its matrix scooped out like the pulp of a fruit and carried away on the endless lines of trucks.

Below the sweeping beams of powerful spotlights, their arcs cutting through the whirling dust, huge pylons were rooted into the black earth, then braced back by hundreds of steel hawsers. In the intervals between them vast steel sheets were erected, welded together to form a continuous windshield a hundred feet high.

Even before the screen was complete the first graders were moving into the sheltered zone behind it, sinking their metal teeth into the bruised earth, levelling out a giant rectangle. Steel forms were shackled into place and scores of black-suited workers moved rapidly like frantic ants, pouring in thousands of gallons of concrete.

As each layer annealed, the forms were unshackled and replaced further up the sloping flanks of the structure. First ten feet, then twenty and thirty feet high, it rose steadily into the dark night.

Chapter 3

Vortex Over London

Deborah Mason took the bundle of teletype dispatches off Andrew Symington's desk, glanced quickly through them and asked, 'Any hopeful news?'

Symington shook his head slowly. Behind him the banks of teletypes – labelled Ankara, Bangkok, Copenhagen and so on through the alphabet – chattered away, churning out endless tapes. They almost filled the small newsroom, cramming the desks of the three-man staff over into a corner.

'Still looks bad, Deborah. Up to 175 now and shows no signs of breaking.' He scrutinized her carefully, noting the lines of tension that webbed the corners of her eyes, gave her smooth, intelligent face a look of precocious maturity, although she was only twenty-five. Unlike most of the girls working at Central Operations Executive, she still kept herself trim and well-groomed. He reflected that the ascendancy of woman in the twentieth century made the possibility of an abrupt end to civilization seem infinitely remote; it was difficult to visualize a sleek young executive like Deborah Mason taking her place in the doomed lifeboats. She was much more the sort of girl who heard the faint SOS signals and organized the rescue operations.

Which, of course, was exactly what she was doing at Central Operations Executive. With the slight difference that this time the whole world was in the last lifeboat. But with people like Deborah and Simon Marshall, the COE intelligence chief, working the pumps, there was a good chance of success.

The unit, directly responsible to the Prime Minister, had

been formed only two weeks previously. Staffed largely by War Office personnel, with a few communications specialists such as Symington recruited from the Air Ministry and industry, its job was to act as an intelligence section handling and sorting all incoming information, and also to serve as the executive agency of the Combined Chiefs of Staff and the Home Office. Its headquarters were situated in the old Admiralty buildings in Whitehall, a rambling network of stately boardrooms and tiny offices in the underground bunkers deep below Horseguards Parade. Here Symington spent most of the day and night, only getting back to his wife – who was expecting her baby within a fortnight at the outside – usually after she was asleep. Along with the wives and families of the other COE personnel, she was housed in the Park Lane Hotel, which had been taken over by the government. Symington saw her daily, and as one of the few employees not resident at the Admiralty he was able to verify personally the reports he spent all day preparing.

TOKYO: 174 mph. 99 per cent of the city down. Explosive fires from Mitsubashi steelworks spreading over western suburbs. Casualties estimated at 15,000. Food and water adequate for three days. Government action confined to police patrols.

ROME: 176 mph. Municipal and office buildings still intact, but Vatican roofless, dome of St Peter's destroyed. Casualties: 2,000. Suburbs largely derelict. Refugees from rural areas flooding into city, catacombs requisitioned by government for relief and dormitories.

NEW YORK: 175 mph. All skyscrapers in Manhattan windowless and abandoned. TV aerial and tower of Empire State Building down. Statue of Liberty minus head and torch. Torrential seas breaking inshore as far as Central Park. City at standstill. Casualties: 500.

VENICE: 176 mph. City abandoned. Casualties: 2,000. Heavy seas have demolished Grand Canal palazzos. St Mark's Square under water, campanile down. All inhabitants on mainland.

ARCHANGEL: 68 mph. No casualties. Intact. Airfield and harbour closed.

CAPE TOWN: 74 mph. 4 casualties. Intact.

SINGAPORE: 178 mph. City abandoned. Government control non-existent. Casualties: 25,000.

Simon Marshall read carefully through the reports, chewed his lip for a moment and then gave them to Deborah to file.

'Not so good, but not so bad either. Tokyo and Singapore, of course, are gone, but one can't expect those cardboard jungles to stand up to winds above hurricane force. Pity about Venice.'

A large powerful man of fifty, with a tough handsome face, strong arms and shoulders, Marshall filled the big office, sitting massively at his desk like an intelligent bear. He had built up COE in little more than two weeks, hiring and firing the necessary personnel single-handed, organizing a world-wide coverage of reporters, seizing the services of top meteorological, communications and electronics experts. COE now was one of the Western Hemisphere's key nerve centres, keeping the Combined Chiefs of Staffs and the government as well informed as they could be.

'Get home all right last night?' he asked Deborah.

'Yes, thanks.' She glanced at her wrist watch. It was 10.57, three minutes before Marshall was to give his daily report to the Combined Chiefs, but he had already mastered the entire intelligence picture, was completely relaxed.

As the minute hand of the clock moved on to 10.59, Marshall stood up and left his desk. The meeting took place in the cabinet room at the end of the corridor. As Deborah picked up Marshall's briefcase, he took it from her with a smile, his hand pressed over hers as he held the handle. The other hand touched her waist, pushed her gently towards the door.

'Time for our tête-à-tête,' he said. 'Let's see if we can give them something today to keep them happy.'

The other members of the COE cabinet were taking their seats as they entered. There were five members, who reported to the Prime Minister through Sir Charles Gort, Permanent Secretary at the Home Office. A trim neat figure in pin-striped trousers and dark jacket, he was a professional civil servant, quiet but firmly spoken, never appearing to volunteer an opinion of his own but adept at reconciling contrary viewpoints.

He waited for the others to settle down, and then turned to Dr Lovatt Dickinson, Director of the Meteorological Office, a sandy-haired Scot in a brown tweed suit, who sat on his left.

'Doctor, perhaps you'd be good enough to let us have the latest news on the weather front.'

Dickinson sat forward, reading from a pad of blue Meteorological Office tabular memos.

'Well, Sir Charles, I can't say that I've anything very hopeful to report. The wind speed is now 175 miles per hour, an increase of 4.89 miles per hour over the speed recorded at 10 a.m. yesterday, maintaining the average daily increase of five miles per hour that we've seen over the last three weeks. The humidity shows a slight increase, to be accounted for by the passage of these enormous air volumes over the disturbed ocean surfaces. We've done our best to make high-altitude observations, but you'll appreciate that launching a balloon in this wind, let alone keeping track of it, is well nigh impossible. However, the weather ship *Northern Survey* off the coast of Greenland, where the wind speed is down to a mere eighty-five mph, has reported data indicating, as one would expect, that the velocity of the global air stream declines with decreasing density, and that at 45,000 feet the air speed is approximately forty-five mph at the equator and thirty mph over this latitude.'

Dickinson momentarily lost his sequence, and while he shuffled the memos Gort cut in smoothly.

'Thank you, Doctor. But boiling it all down, what prospects are there of the wind system's actually subsiding?'

Dickinson shook his head dourly. 'I'd like to be optimistic, Sir Charles, but I've every suspicion that it's got some way to go yet before it spends itself. We're witnessing a meteorological phenomenon of unprecedented magnitude, a global cyclone accelerating at a uniform rate, exhibiting all the signs distinguishing highly stable aerodynamic systems. The wind mass now has tremendous momentum, and the inertial forces alone will prevent a sudden abatement.

'Theoretically there are no reasons why it should not continue to revolve at high speeds indefinitely, and become the prevailing planetary system similar to the revolving clouds of gas that produce the rings of Saturn. To date the weather systems on this planet have always been dictated by the oceanic drifts, but it's obvious now that far stronger influences are at work. Exactly what, any of you are free to speculate.

'Recently our monitors have detected unusually high levels of cosmic radiation. All electromagnetic wave forms have mass – perhaps a vast tangential stream of cosmic radiation exploded from the sun during the solar eclipse a month ago, struck the earth on one exposed hemisphere, and its gravitational drag might have set in motion the huge cyclone revolving round the earth's axis at this moment.'

Dickinson looked around the table and smiled sombrely. 'Or again, maybe it's the deliberate act of an outraged Providence, determined to sweep man and his pestilence from the surface of this once green earth. Who can say?'

Gort pursed his lips, eyeing Dickinson with dry amusement. 'Well, let's sincerely hope not, Doctor. We simply haven't got a big enough budget for that sort of emergency.

Summing up, then, it looks as if we were optimistic a week ago when we assumed, quite naturally, that the wind would exhaust itself once it reached the hurricane force. We can expect it to continue, if not indefinitely, at least for a considerable period, perhaps another month. Could we now have a report of the present position as assessed by the intelligence section?'

Marshall sat forward, the eyes of the other men at the table turning towards him.

'Recapping for a moment, Sir Charles, it's exactly eight days since London first began to experience winds of over 120 miles an hour, greater than any previously recorded, and certainly well beyond anything the architects of this city designed for. Bearing that in mind, I'm sure you'll be proud to hear that our great capital city is holding together with remarkable tenacity.' Marshall glanced around the table, letting the impact of this homily sink in, then continued in a slightly more factual tone:

'Taking London first, although almost all activity in the commercial and industrial sense has ceased for the time being, the majority of people are getting by without too much difficulty. Most of them have managed to board up their houses, secure their roofs, and lay in adequate stocks of food and water. Casualties have been low – 2,000 – and many of these were elderly people who were probably frightened to death, quite literally, rather than injured by falling masonry.'

Marshall glanced through his notes. 'Abroad, in Europe and North America, the picture is pretty much the same. They've all battened down the hatches and are ready to ride out the storm. Scandinavia and northern Russia, of course, are outside the main wind belt and life seems to be going on much as usual. They're equipped for hurricane-force winds as a matter of course.' Marshall smiled his big craggy smile. 'I think we can probably stand another twenty or thirty mph without any real damage.'

Major-General Harris, a small man in a spic-and-span uniform, nodded briskly.

'Good to hear you say that, Marshall. Morale isn't as high as it could be. Too much negative talk around.'

Vice-Admiral Saunders, sitting next to him, nodded agreement.

'I hope your information is right, though, Marshall. One of the Americans told me this morning that Venice was a complete write-off.'

'Exaggeration,' Marshall said easily. 'My latest report a few minutes ago was that there had been heavy flooding, but no serious damage.'

The admiral nodded, glad to be reassured. Marshall continued with his survey. Deborah sat just behind him, listening to the steady confident tone. With the exception of Gort, who remained neutral, the three other members of the committee were inclined to be pessimistic and depressed, expecting the worst and misinterpreting the news to serve their unconscious acceptance of disaster. General Harris and Vice-Admiral Saunders were typical of the sort of serviceman in the saddle at the beginning of a war. They had the Dunkirk mentality, had already been defeated and were getting ready to make a triumph out of it, counting up the endless casualty lists, the catalogues of disaster and destruction, as if these were a measure of their courage and competence.

Marshall, Deborah realized, was the necessary counterforce on the team. Although he might be over-optimistic, this was deliberate, the sort of Churchillian policy that would keep people head-up into the wind, doing everything to defend themselves, rather than running helplessly before it. She listened half consciously to Marshall, feeling his confidence surge through her.

On the way back to Marshall's office after the meeting closed, they met Symington, carrying a teletype memo in his hand.

'Bad news, I'm afraid, sir. The old Russell Square Hotel collapsed suddenly about half an hour ago. Some of the piles drove straight through the sub-soil into the Piccadilly Line platforms directly below. First estimates are that about two hundred were killed in the Russell basement and about twice that number again in the station.'

Marshall took the tape and stared at it blindly for several moments, bunching his fist and drumming it against his forehead.

'Deborah, get this out to all casualty units straight away! About four hundred were down in the station, you say, Andrew? For God's sake, what were they doing there? Don't tell me they were waiting for a train.'

Symington gestured with one hand. 'I suppose they were sheltering there, the way they did in World War II.'

In a burst of exasperation, Marshall shouted: 'But that's just what we don't want them to do! They should have been above ground, strengthening their own homes, not just abandoning them and cowering away like a lot of sheep.'

Symington smiled wanly. 'Properties in the Bloomsbury and Russell Square area are pretty decrepit. High Victorian terraced houses ready for demolition. People there live in single rooms –'

'I don't care where they live!' Marshall cut in. 'There are eight million people in this city and they've got to stand up and face this wind together. Once they start thinking of themselves and a warm hole to hide in the whole damn place will blow away.'

He swung through into his office. 'Call transport,' he snapped at Deborah. 'Tell them to get a car ready. We'll go out and have a look at this ourselves.'

He pulled a heavy trench coat off the door, climbed into it while Deborah hurried over to the phone. As he strode off down the corridor she followed, slipping into her own coat.

The operations deck was on the second floor of the Admiralty building, a honeycomb of small partitioned offices off the narrow high-ceilinged corridors. They passed the overseas news section, made their way through into a wide office which was the UK news reception unit. There were a dozen teletypes taping down an endless stream of information from the major provincial capitals, TV screens flickering with pictures broadcast from mobile transmitter units all over London, and a trio of operators in direct touch with the Met. Office.

'What are the latest casualties at Russell Square?' Marshall asked a young lieutenant sitting at a desk in front of a TV set, watching the screen as he talked rapidly into a boom mike jutting from his shoulder.

'Heavy, I'm afraid, sir. At least four hundred dead. The station access platforms are in pitch darkness, and they're waiting for the RASC unit at Liverpool Street Station to move their generator down.'

The screen was blurred and indistinct, but Marshall could make out the stabbing beams of searchlights playing over the ragged silhouette of the collapsed hotel. Its ten storeys had concertinaed to the equivalent of three; many of the windows and balconies were apparently intact, but closer inspection revealed that the floors were separated by an interval of only three or four feet instead of the usual twelve.

Marshall took Deborah's arm and led her out of the room into the corridor. They walked down the stairs to the ground floor. The building was equipped with its own generator but its power was inadequate to move the heavy elevator.

All the windows they passed were securely boarded. Outside, ten-foot-thick walls of sandbags had been stacked up to the roof, roped into an impenetrable wall. As they neared the ground floor, however, Deborah felt the building shudder slightly as a massive draught of air struck it, stirring the foundations in their clay beds. The movement stabbed at her heart, and she stopped for a moment and leaned against

Marshall. He put an arm around her shoulders, smiled reassuringly.

'All right, Deborah?' His hand cupped the round swell of her shoulder through the jacket.

'Just about. I'm afraid it startled me.'

They moved down the steps, Marshall slowing his pace for her. The tremor continued as the building settled itself into new foundations.

'Something big must have come down,' Marshall said. 'Probably the Palace, or No. 10 Downing Street.' He gave a light laugh.

At the bottom of the steps there was a revolving door, heavy rubber flaps making the seal airtight. Inside the building the air was filtered, the suites of offices and the operations deck contained in a warm, noiseless world. Beyond the revolving doors, however, in the corridors leading to the transport bay and the service units, the air seeped in through the casing of sandbags, driven by the tremendous pressure of the wind outside, and through the glass panels of the revolving doors they could see the floor, thick with dust and grime, chilled by sudden gusts of air bursting through pressure points.

Marshall put up his collar, led them briskly down the corridor to an orderly room by the rear exit, where he collected their driver. Five or six exhausted men in dirty khaki uniforms sat around a table drinking tea. Their faces looked pinched and sallow. For three weeks now no one had seen the sun; the dust clouds dimmed the streets, turned noon into a winter evening.

Marshall's driver, a small wiry corporal called Musgrave, unlocked a narrow panel door in the steel blast-proof bulkhead at the end of the corridor. Deborah and Marshall followed him into a low-ceilinged garage where three armoured cars were parked. They were M53-pattern Bethlehems, square ten-ton vehicles with canted armoured sides designed originally to deflect high-velocity shells and now ideal shielding for surface units moving about in the wind. Their 85 mm. guns had been removed, and in place of the original mounting six-inch-thick perspex window pieces had been fastened.

After helping Deborah into the truck, Marshall followed, swinging himself up in two easy powerful movements. Musgrave tested the hatch, then climbed into the driver's seat beside the engine and pulled the hatch over himself.

He drove the car forward across the garage floor, and edged it up onto the wide steel plate of a hydraulically operated elevator shaft. Remote controlled from the car's radio, the elevator rose slowly into the air on its single pylon, carrying the car upward into a narrow well in the roof of the garage. As it neared the top the roof retracted sideways, and the Bethlehem emerged into the rear courtyard, between Admiralty House and the Foreign Office Annex.

Inside the cabin, Marshall sat on the edge of the padded metal seat, craning forward into the circular window. Deborah crouched behind him, switching on the radio channel to the Operations Room.

They made their way into Trafalgar Square, turned up the west side towards the National Gallery. It was one o'clock but the air was dark and grey, the sky overcast. Only the continuously flickering tracerlike striations across the air gave any indication of the air stream's enormous speed. They reached Canada House and the Cunard building on the west side of the square, and the walls of sandbags and the exposed cornices above flickered with the violent impact of the dust clouds.

Nelson's Column was down. Two weeks earlier, when the wind had reached ninety-five mph, a crack which had passed unnoticed for seventy-five years suddenly revealed itself a third of the way up the shaft. The next day the upper section had toppled, the shattered cylindrical segments still lying where they had fallen among the four bronze lions.

The square was deserted. Along the north side a tunnel

of sandbags ran from the Haymarket and turned up into Charing Cross Road. Only military personnel and police used these covered runways; everyone else was indoors, refusing to venture out until the wind abated. The new office blocks along the Strand and the clubs along Pall Mall were heavily sandbagged and looked as if they had been abandoned by their occupants to sustain alone the terrors of some apocalyptic air raid. Most of the smaller office buildings had been left unprotected, however, and their windows had been stripped away, their floors and ceilings gutted.

As they turned into Charing Cross Road Marshall noted that the Garrick Theatre had collapsed. The unsupported auditorium walls had caved in completely, and the arcs of the dress and upper circles now looked down onto a wind-swept pile of rubble. The lines of seats were being stripped away like dominoes. Marshall watched them explode off their moorings and cannonade out into the street, as if jerked away on the end of enormous hawsers, disintegrating as they flew.

As they moved up Shaftesbury Avenue towards Holborn, Marshall waved Deborah forward and she joined him and rested her elbows on the traverse. In the dim light of the cabin she could see the strong edge of Marshall's jaw and forehead illuminated in profile. For some reason he was undeterred by the immense force of the wind.

He put his hand over hers. 'Frightened, Deborah?'

She moved her fingers, held his hand tightly. 'I'm not just frightened, Simon. Staring out here – it's like looking onto a city of hell. Everything's so totally uncertain, and I'm sure this isn't the end.'

Searchlights played across Kingsway as they crossed the road, shone into the observation window and momentarily dazzled them. The Bethlehem halted at the intersection while Musgrave spoke to the command post dug into the mouth of Holborn Underground Station. Ahead, along

Southampton Row, was a group of vehicles – three Centurion tanks, each pulling a steel trailer.

Musgrave joined them, and together the column moved slowly up towards Russell Square. More vehicles were drawn up by the collapsed hotel, others were moving about in the square, their tracks flattening the tattered remains of the few bushes and shreds of wire fencing that still protruded from the beaten ground. Two Bethlehems with RN insignia were up on the edge of the pavement in front of the hotel, playing their searchlights onto the jumble of telescoped floors.

They moved around the block to the windward side. Here a line of Centurion tanks was drawn up, sandbags piled between them, steel hoods mounted on their track guards locked end to end to form a windshield, giving the rescue squads digging their way into the basement sufficient protection to move around. Their success was hard to assess, but Marshall realized that few survivors could be expected. The heavy rescue rigs – all originally designed and built for World War II and now pulled out of their mothballs – needed more freedom of movement. There were huge draglines, mounted on tracks as high as a man, fitted with hinged booms that could reach between two telescoped floors. One of them was feeling its way tentatively below the buckled lintels of the second floor like a giant hand reaching into a deep pocket, but the wind sent it slamming from side to side, and the crew in their armoured cab found it impossible to control.

Musgrave drove the Bethlehem up onto the opposite pavement, and they edged past the line of vehicles to where a massive tractor, almost as big as a house, sixty-foot-long steel booms jutting up from its front like the twin jibs of a sailing ship, was edging a circular steel escape shaft into position. The shaft pivoted between the booms. The lower end drove through a narrow window below the edge of the pavement, then powerful hydraulic rams extended it downward into the matrix of the ruin. Inside the shaft rescue teams equipped with steel props would spread out across the basement, crawling along the foot-high space that was probably all that was left of the floor.

Next to it were two more tracked vehicles, fitted with conveyor belts that carried an endless stream of rubble away from the ruin and dumped them onto the roadway behind. Some of the fragments of masonry were six feet long – massive blocks of fractured concrete that weighed half a ton.

'If there's anyone alive in there they'll find them,' Marshall said to Deborah. Just then the Bethlehem slid into reverse and backed suddenly, throwing them against the traverse. Marshall swore, holding his left elbow, the arm paralyzed for a moment. Deborah had struck her forehead against the steel rim. She pushed herself away and Marshall was about to go to her aid when he heard Musgrave jabber excitedly over the intercom.

'Look out, sir! The conveyor's going over!'

Marshall leaped to the window. The wind had caught one of the two conveyors, swung the thirty-foot-high escalator around like a balsawood dummy. The huge vehicle swivelled helplessly. Its tracks tautened as the twin diesels pulled, and the driver backed the whole unit away from the ruin, trying to regain its balance. Moving in a sharp arc, it backed straight towards the opposite pavement, where the Bethlehem had stalled with its rear wheels jammed against the steps of one of the houses.

Before they collided the conveyor driver saw the Bethlehem in his rear mirror and retroversed the tracks, the great steel cleats stabbing through the surface of the roadway, locking in a sudden spasm. Immediately the twenty grab buckets swung back and inverted, tipping their contents into the roadway below.

A fragment of masonry fifteen feet long, a virtually intact section of balcony, fell straight onto the hood of the Bethlehem. The car slammed down onto its front axle, rear wheels bouncing off the pavement. Arms shielding his head, Marshall was hurled around the cabin, Deborah knocked off her feet. When the car finally steadied he bent down over Deborah and helped her off the floor onto the seat.

The front suspension of the Bethlehem had collapsed and the floor tilted downward. Marshall leaned over, peered through the window, and saw the long slab of concrete which straddled the hood, its lower edge penetrating the driver's hatchway.

'Musgrave!' Marshall bellowed into the intercom. 'Musgrave! Are you all right, man?'

He dropped the mike, bent down under the traverse and wrenched back the radio set, hammering on the hinged panel that sealed off the cabin from the driver's compartment. Musgrave had locked it from his side. Marshall tore at the edges of the panel, managed to pull the one-eighth inch plate back off its louvers. Through the crack he could see the hunched form of the driver. He had slipped off his seat, was stuffed head down into the narrow interval below the driving columns.

Marshall pulled himself to his feet, climbed up onto the edge of the traverse and unlocked the hatch bars. Deborah jumped up and tried to hold him back, but he shouldered her off and punched the hatch sections up into the air. Air whirled into the cabin, gusts of stinging dust carried down from the ruined hotel. Hesitating for a moment, Marshall heaved himself up into the air, head and trunk out of the hatch.

Immediately the wind caught him and jack-knifed him over the edge of the turret. For a few seconds he hung there, pinned by the wind stream, then pulled himself downward and spilled onto the ground, driven back against the underside of the chassis. The wind drove under his coat, splitting down his back and then stripping the two sections off his arms like a piece of rotten cotton ripped in two. He watched them blow away, then dragged himself along the side of the car, hand over hand, by the camouflage-netting hasps rivetted along the bottom of the chassis.

A continuous shower of stones drove over him, slashing red welts across his hands and neck. The tall houses facing the hotel deflected the wind slightly and he managed to reach the hood of the Bethlehem. Anchoring himself between the tyre and hood, he stretched out painfully to the concrete beam, bunching every muscle as he strained against its massive weight. Through the swirling half light the huge rescue vehicles loomed over the hotel like armoured mastodons feeding on an enormous corpse.

He pressed against the beam, hopelessly trying to lift it, his eyes blacking out momentarily, then slumped down against the tyre just as two Centurions approached the Bethlehem, their steel shutters extended. They swung around the car, locked shields and drove in together, immediately lifting the wind stream off Marshall. A third tractor, an armoured bulldozer, backed up to the Bethlehem and swung its ram over the cabin and down onto the hood. Expertly retroversing his tracks, the driver flipped the concrete beam off the Bethlehem, then drove off.

Marshall tried to climb up onto the hood, but his leg and back muscles were useless. Two men in vinyl uniforms leaped down from the Centurions. One swarmed up onto the car, opened the driver's hatch and slid inside. The other took Marshall by the arm, helped him up onto the turret and into the cabin.

While Marshall sat back limply against the radio, the man ran expert fingers over him, wiping the welts across his face with an antiseptic sponge he pulled from his first-aid kit. Finally he propped Marshall's swollen hands on his knees and turned to Deborah, who knelt beside Marshall, trying to clean his face with her handkerchief.

'Relax, he's in one piece.' He pointed to the radio. 'Get me channel four, will you? We'll give you a tow back. One of the front tyres is flat.'

While Deborah fumbled at the console he looked down at Marshall, lolling against the cabin wall, his great head like a weathered rock, shoulders flexing as he gasped for air. A network of fine blue veins webbed his cheeks and forehead, giving the powerful lines of his face a steely sheen.

Deborah selected the channel, passed the mike across.

'Maitland here. Marshall is O.K. I'll ride back with him just in case he tries to climb out again. How's the driver? Sorry about him. . . . Can you get him out? All right, then, seal him in and they can cut him loose later.'

Maitland reached up and secured the hatch, then sat back against the traverse and pulled off his helmet and goggles. Marshall leaned forward weakly, elbows on his knees, feeling the swollen veins across his face.

'Air bruises,' Maitland told him. 'Minute haemorrhages. They'll be all over your back and chest. Take a few days to clear.'

He smiled at them as Deborah crouched down beside Marshall, putting her arm around his shoulders, and smoothed his hair back with her small hands.

They reached Marshall's house in Park Lane in half an hour, towed by one of the Centurions. High steel gates let them into a small covered courtyard where two of Marshall's guards disconnected the tank and then rolled the Bethlehem down a long ramp into the basement. Maitland helped Marshall out of the turret. The big man had begun to recover. He limped slowly across the concrete floor, the sole of one of his shoes flapping, holding the remnants of his suit around him, his hand taking Deborah's arm.

As they waited for the elevator he turned to Maitland, gave him a craggy smile.

'Thanks, Doctor. It was stupid of me, but the poor devil was dying only a couple of feet away, and I couldn't do a damn thing to help him.'

One of the guards opened the doors and they stepped through and were carried up to Marshall's suite on the first floor. All the windows had been bricked in. From the street Marshall's house appeared to be imitation Georgian, slender lintels over high narrow windows, but the façade was skin deep, slung on a heavy steel superstructure that carried the wind easily. The air in the suite was quiet and filtered, hanging motionlessly over the purple carpeting – one of the few private oases that still existed in London.

They entered Marshall's drawing-room, a two-level room with a circular black glass staircase. Below, an open log fire burned in a massive fireplace, throwing a soft flickering glow onto the semicircular couch in front of it, reflecting off the black tiles and the lines of silver trophies in their cases against the wall. The room was expensively and carefully furnished, with a strong masculine taste. There were abstract statuettes; heavy sporting rifles clipped to the walls, their black barrels glinting; a small winged bull rearing from a dark corner, its hooded eyes blind and menacing. Altogether the effect was powerful, a perfect image of Marshall's own personality, intense and somehow disturbing.

Marshall slumped down onto the sofa, leaving the lights off. Deborah watched him for a moment, then slipped out of her coat and went over to the cocktail cabinet. She poured whisky into a glass, then splashed in soda and brought the drink over to Marshall, sitting down on the sofa next to him.

He took it from her, then reached out and put his hand on her thigh. Tucking her legs under her, she moved close to him and began to stroke his cheek and forehead with her finger tips, feeling the fine tracery of contused veins.

'I'm sorry about Musgrave,' she said. Marshall's hand rested in her lap, warm and strong. She took the glass from him and sipped at it, feeling the hot fiery liquid burn down her throat, brilliant and stimulating.

'Poor devil,' Marshall commented. 'Those Bethlehems

68

are useless; the armour is too thin to hold a falling building.'
To himself he added: 'Hardoon will want something
tougher.'

'Who?' Deborah asked. She had come across the name
somewhere else before. 'Who's Hardoon?'

Marshall waved airily. 'Just one of the people I'm dealing
with.' He took his eyes off the fire and looked up at Deborah.
Her face was only a few inches from his own, her eyes wide
and steady, an expectant smile on her full lips.

'You were saying something about the Bethlehems,' she
said quietly, massaging his cheeks with the knuckle of her
forefinger.

Marshall smiled admiringly. Cool passionate lover,
he thought. I must try to remember to take you with me.

'Yes, we need something heavier. The wind's going to
blow a lot harder.'

As he spoke Deborah moved her face against his, then
brushed her lips softly across his forehead, murmuring to
herself.

Reflectively, Marshall finished his drink, then put it down
and took her in both arms.

Maitland watched as the acetylene torch cut neatly
through the steel buttress over the driving cabin. The whole
section slipped slightly, and he helped the two mechanics
raise it over the hood and put it down on the floor of the
garage. Musgrave's body was still lying bunched up below
the dashboard. He leaned over the wheel and felt for the
pulse, then signalled the other two to lift it out.

They carried the driver over to a bench, stretched him
out. A guard came out of the radio-control booth and walked
over to Maitland. He was a tough, hard-faced man of
indeterminate background, wearing the same black uniform
as all Marshall's personnel. Maitland wondered how large
his private army was. The three members he had seen were

obviously recruited independently; there were no service or rank tags on their shoulders and they treated the Bethlehem and himself as intruders.

'There's a big navy crawler on its way down from Hampstead,' the guard told Maitland curtly. 'They'll tow you back to the Green Park base.'

Maitland nodded. He felt suddenly tired and looked around for somewhere to sit. The one bench was occupied by Musgrave's body, so he squatted down on the floor against a ventilator shaft, listening to the wind drumming in the street outside. Now and then the blades of the fan stopped and reversed as a pressure pulse drove down the shaft, then picked up and sped on again.

Apart from the Bethlehem there was only one other vehicle in the basement, a long double-tracked armoured trailer being loaded by two guards from a freight lift. They brought up an endless succession of wooden crates, some loaded into the lift so rapidly that their lids were still waiting to be nailed down.

Out of curiosity, Maitland wandered over to the carrier when the guards had gone down in the lift. He assumed the crates would be full of expensive furniture and tableware, and looked under one of the loose lids.

Packed into the crates were six $3\frac{1}{2}$ inch trench mortars, their wide green barrels thick with protective grease.

The mortars were War Department issues, but there was no clearance seal on the sides of the crate listing their destination and authority. Turning the lid over, Maitland saw that it had been stamped in black dye: 'Breathing apparatus. Hardoon Tower.'

Most of the other cases were sealed, stamped variously with markings that identified them as oxyacetylene cylinders, trenching equipment, flares and pit props. Another open case, marked 'Denims. Hardoon Tower,' contained a neatly stowed collection of the black uniforms he had seen Marshall's men wearing. Hardoon Tower, Maitland pondered.

He repeated the name to himself, trying to identify it, then remembered a newspaper profile he had read years earlier about the eccentric multimillionaire who owned vast construction interests and had built an elaborate underground bunker city on his estate near London at the height of the cold war.

'O.K., Doctor?'

He swung round to see the big tough-faced guard who had arranged his transport step slowly across the floor, arms swinging loosely at his sides. Whether he was armed was hard to tell, but his battledress jacket could have hidden a weapon.

Maitland tapped the case full of trench mortars. 'Just looking at this – breathing apparatus. Unusual design.'

The guard scowled. 'That's a useful piece of equipment, Doctor. Very versatile. Let's go, then.' As Maitland walked back across the basement the guard pivoted on one heel and followed close to his shoulder.

'What's Marshall trying to do?' Maitland asked amiably. 'Start a war?'

The guard watched Maitland thoughtfully. 'Don't know what we might start. But let's not get too worried about it, Doctor. Sit down over there and take your pulse or something.'

They wrapped Musgrave in a polythene shroud and lowered him into the turret of the Bethlehem. Maitland climbed in and wedged the body below the traverse, belting it down with the seat straps.

When he tried to get out he found that someone was sitting on the hatch, his feet obscuring the plexiglass window. For a moment he wondered whether to force it, then decided to take the hint. A few minutes later the navy crawler arrived and backed down the ramp. He felt it hook up to the Bethlehem, then move forward up into the street.

Powerful gusts of wind drove at the car, kicking it around.

He gripped the traverse, swaying from side to side as the cabin plunged and bucked.

All around him, in the streets outside, he could hear the sounds of falling masonry.

Chapter 4

The Corridors of Pain

Three times, on the way back to the Green Park depot, the car left the roadway. Caught by tremendous cross-winds that swung it about behind the Centurion like a hapless tail, the Bethlehem plunged across the pavement, almost tipping over onto its side.

The streets were full of rubble and pieces of masonry, fragments of ornamented cornices from the older buildings, the remains of roof timbers strewn across the pavement, everywhere a heavy autumnlike fall of grey tiles.

They reached the depot at Green Park which housed Combined Rescue Operations, and entered the long tunnel of concrete sandbags that led them into the covered transport pool. A dozen other vehicles, Centurions and Bethlehems with a couple of huge M5 Titan personnel carriers, were unloading and refuelling. Three of them had RN insignia; the navy, to whom Maitland was attached, shared the depot, but all the personnel in the pool wore the same drab uniforms. They looked tired and dispirited, and Maitland found himself sharing their despair. As he climbed out of the Bethlehem he leaned for a few minutes against the car, trying to free himself of the muscle and mind numbing weariness from the buffeting he had received all day.

He de-briefed himself quickly, then made his way towards the officers' quarters where he shared a small cubicle with a navy surgeon called Avery. Eager for a full role in the emergency, particularly with the RAF playing no part, the navy had put together a scratch operations unit. With Andrew Symington's help, Maitland had been assimilated with a minimum of formality. He had stayed with Andrew and his wife for a week, uselessly waiting for the wind to subside, and had been glad to be given a chance to do something positive.

Maitland closed the door and sat down wearily on his bed, grunting to Avery, who was stretched out full length, his black wind suit unzipped.

'Hello, Donald. What's it like outside?'

Maitland shrugged. 'A slight east wind blowing up.' He took a cigarette from the silver case Avery passed to him. 'I've been over at the Russell most of today. Not too pleasant. Looks like a foretaste of things to come. I hope everybody knows what they're doing.'

Avery grunted. 'Of course they don't. Reminds me of Mark Twain's crack about the weather – everyone talks about it, but no one does anything.' He rolled over and switched on the portable radio standing on the floor below his bed. A fuzzy crackle sounded out eventually, almost drowned in the noise of people continually tramping up and down the corridor.

Maitland lay back, listening to phrases from the news bulletins. The BBC was still transmitting on the Home Service, half-hourly news summaries interspersed with light music and an apparently endless stream of War Office orders and recommendations. So far the government appeared to be tacitly assuming that the wind would soon spend itself and that most people possessed sufficient food and water to survive unaided in their own homes. The majority of the troops were engaged in laying communications tunnels, repairing electricity lines and reinforcing their own installations.

Avery switched the set off and sat up on one elbow for a moment, staring pensively at his wrist watch.

'What's the latest?' Maitland asked.

Avery smiled sombrely. 'Lanyon Bridge is falling down,' he said quietly. 'Wind speed's up to 180. Listening between the lines, it sounds as if things are getting pretty bad. Colossal flooding along the south coast – most of Brighton sounds as if it's been washed away. General chaos building up everywhere. What I want to know is, when are they going to start doing something?'

'What can they do?'

Avery gestured impatiently. 'For God's sake, you know what I mean, Donald. They're going about the whole thing the wrong way, just telling people to stay indoors and hide under the staircase. What do they think this is – a zeppelin raid? They're going to have the most fantastic casualties soon. Let alone a couple of typhoid and cholera epidemics.'

Maitland nodded. He agreed with Avery but felt too tired to offer any comment.

There was a familiar tattoo on the door, and Andrew Symington put his head in. He was off duty at eight, and came over in the communications tunnel across St James's Park to take his meals in the civilian mess at the depot before going over to the Park Lane Hotel. His wife's baby had still not arrived, at least a fortnight overdue. Dora was unconsciously holding the child to herself.

'We were just cursing these damn silly bulletins you people are putting out,' Avery said. 'Are you trying to convince yourself it's a calm summer's day?'

'What's the real news, Andrew?' Maitland pressed. 'I got in half an hour ago and it sounded as if the Russell wasn't the only place coming down.'

'It isn't,' Symington told him. His face looked drawn and tired. He lit a cigarette, inhaled quickly. 'Everything I've heard indicates that we can expect the wind strength to go on increasing for several days more at least. Apparently localized areas of turbulence have to appear first while the overall wind strength continues to increase, and they've shown no signs of doing so. Whatever happens, it's bound to go up another fifty at least.'

Avery whistled. 'Over 230! God Almighty.' He tapped

the wooden wall partition which was springing backward and forward as air pressed its way past. 'Do you think this place will stand it?'

'This building probably will, even if it loses the roof, but already most of the domestic houses in the British Isles are starting to come down. Roofs are flying off, walls caving in – not all that many modern houses are fitted with basements. People are running out of food, trying to leave their homes to reach the aid stations. They're being sucked out of their doorways before they know what's hit them, carried half a mile within ten seconds.' Symington paused. 'We aren't getting much news in now from the States and western Europe, but you can imagine what the Far East looks like. Governmental control no longer exists. Most of the radio stations are just putting out weak local identification signals.'

For half an hour they talked, then Symington left them and Maitland slipped off to sleep, still wearing his wind suit. He was vaguely aware of Avery's getting up to go out on duty, then sank into a heavy restless sleep.

Six hours later, as they listened to their briefing in one of the lecture rooms at the far end of the depot, the sounds of collapsing masonry thudded dimly in the distance. The walls shifted uneasily, as if one end of the depot were seized in the mandibles of some enormous insect. An outside wall carrying the stairway up to the roof at the windward end of the barracks had collapsed, dropping the stairway like a pile of plates. Luckily the internal walls that divided the stairway from the remainder of the barracks held long enough for them to extricate themselves and most of their luggage, but five minutes after they retreated to the adjacent building the barracks toppled in a whirling cloud of dust and exploding brickwork.

The captain up on the dais raised his voice above the approaching rumble. 'I'll keep this short so we can get out before the place comes down on our necks. Wind speed's up to 180, and frankly the over-all situation is grim. The big job now is to move as many people as we can to under-ground shelters, and we're pulling out of central London and setting up ten major command posts around the outer circular road. Ours is the US Air Force base at Brandon Hall, near Kingston. The deep bunkers there should give us enough room to get a sick bay with about three hundred beds going. There'll be a Navy transport and rescue unit, and they'll try to move people into all the deep shelters – railway tunnels, factory basements and so on – in the immediate area. It's going to be pretty difficult. Some big new transports coming in from Woolwich are supposed to stand up to five hundred-mile-an-hour gales, but even so we'll only be able to move a small proportion of the people we find, and we'll have to pick those who have food with them. Our own supplies are only good for about three weeks.'

He paused and looked down at the rows of sombre faces. 'I hate to say it, but it looks as if casualties are going to be as high as fifty per cent.'

Maitland repeated the figure to himself, trying to digest it. Impossible, he thought. Twenty-five million people? Surely they would cling to life somewhere, at the bottom of deep ditches, chewing old leaves and grass roots. He listened vaguely as the briefing continued, wondering if these preparations would soon prove as inadequate as the first had been.

They shuffled out and took their places in one of the queues winding down the corridors to the transport pool, listening to the mounting rumble from the streets outside. Gusts of filthy air drove through, and the floorboards below Maitland's feet were thick with dirt. The entire top-soil of the globe was being systematically loosened and windborne. The sky was black with dust.

From the talk near him he filled in his impressions of the crisis. The government, centred in the War Office, were dug into their Whitehall bunkers, communicating by radio with the ring of command stations around London and with similar posts in the provinces. An estimated 1,000,000 men – the three armed services, national guard, civil defence and police – were directly controlled by the government and a good proportion of these were involved in organizing and preparing deep shelters wherever they existed. Only a small fraction, perhaps 200,000, were actually employed in rescue work.

Maitland speculated shrewdly that preparations were now in hand for a final retreat of the COE inner core – government and service chiefs, with a few people such as Marshall – to some secret bastion where survival could be assured for a good deal longer. He had tried to report his discovery at Marshall's Park Lane house, but the senior officers at the depot were too busy to listen to him, and anyway had no authority outside the unit. Besides, Hardoon, with his army of construction workers and fleets of equipment, might well be working for the government.

When he finally slung his suitcase up into one of the half-tracked personnel carriers and climbed in after it, there were only a dozen men left in the depot.

The troop carrier was shunted up against one of the Centurions, the two jibs locked together. Both vehicles were loaded with concrete slabs three feet long and 18 inches thick, canted to exaggerate the original slope of the armour plate and provide the minimum wind resistance.

Maitland settled himself among the kitbags and suitcases and peered out through the narrow glass window, an inch-high slit just behind his head. Only two others were with him; an RAF flight sergeant and a young signals corporal.

After a long wait the engines roared out and they edged forward up the exit ramp. As they neared the end of the ramp the horizontal door was retracted and the 180 mph airstream moving across the flat parade ground lifted the carrier out like an enormous hand, slewing it around under a hail of fist-sized stones. The driver gunned the engine and pulled them back on course, and with the Centurion pulling ahead they moved towards the gateway and then through into Green Park. Maitland looked out at the darkened slopes. Stumps of trees stuck up through the turfless soil, littered with stones, gravel and miscellaneous debris that piled up against the embankment walls like refuse in an abandoned municipal dump.

They stopped just past Hyde Park Corner in the entrance to Knightsbridge. Maitland pressed his face to the window slit, looked out at the dim outlines of the office blocks and apartment buildings in the darkness. All of them were shaking perceptibly, heavy tremors jolting the roadway under the carrier. The roofs had been stripped away and Maitland could see the sky through the open top-floor windows. Many of the upper floors had fallen in. All the small shops and boutiques had been completely gutted, their plate glass smashed, interiors cleaned out to the last hatpin and hair curler.

Swinging to the right of the roadway, on the way dislodging the shell of a Jaguar that had trapped itself in a shopfront and now skittered off ahead of them, they avoided the debris piled across their path and pressed on towards the Brompton Road. As they passed Lowndes Square Maitland craned to look up at his apartment house, counting the floors to his own apartment. The building was still intact, but all its lights were out. As they moved on he wondered what had happened to Susan.

Harrod's department store lay in ruins, brownstone facing tiles lying thickly across the roadway, the wind picking like a thousand vultures at the tangle of girders and masonry, detaching fragments of furniture and tattered drapery and carrying them away in its fleeting clasp.

Shaking his head ruefully, Maitland left the window and searched for his cigarettes. He was taking out the pack when the half-track braked sharply. For a moment it hesitated and then began to tip backward and rolled slowly down a shallow incline that had opened in the roadway under the rear section of the vehicle.

Above the din of the wind Maitland could hear the driver shouting into his radio. He felt the Centurion throw its engine into a lower gear, trying to pull them out of the subsidence. The weight of the carrier had apparently caved in a shallow sewer traversing the road. Tilting at a ten-degree angle, the carrier's tracks raced and skated. Gradually it slid helplessly down the incline, pulling the Centurion after it. Finally it rooted itself immovably. The driver raced his engine, flogging the gears like a maniac, while the Centurion jerked and thrust helplessly. Then both engines stopped, and for a few minutes the drivers bellowed into their microphones.

Through the window Maitland could see the sides of a six-foot-deep ditch. Behind was the ragged edge of the asphalt roadway, ahead the massive outline of the tank, its rear track wheels still on the road.

The driver opened his communicating door and came swarming aft, furious with what had happened, waving his arms and shouting: 'Off, off, off! Don't sit here like a lot of helpless sheep.'

The flight sergeant bridled, wondering whether to pull his rank on the corporal, then thought better of it.

'What do we do now, mate?' he asked.

The driver kicked the suitcases out of the way, shouted scornfully, 'Walk, what else? I'm bloody well not going to carry you back!'

He unlocked the rear doors, pushed them open. The Centurion switched on its rear lights, flooding the interior of the carrier. To the left on the pavement above, Maitland could see the grey humped back of a pedestrian tunnel. Part of it had collapsed into the ditch, affording a convenient access point. The driver pointed to it.

'Take that back to Knightsbridge Underground,' he

barked at them. 'Follow the Piccadilly Line to Hammersmith and you'll be picked up there. Got it?'

Maitland hesitated, then began to crawl along the bottom of the ditch towards the aperture in the tunnel. The wind drove overhead like an express train, sucking at the low-pressure space in the road, and he clung to the damp soil like a limpet. Reaching the tunnel, he pulled himself in, then helped the others who came after him.

When they were all inside they saw the Centurion roar into life and move sharply away from the ditch, its lights flashing, then swing round and drive off down the street.

The tunnel had originally been six feet high, but the wind pressure and the successive shells of reinforcing materials added during the past week had lowered the ceiling to little more than five feet off the ground. Here and there, at fifty-yard intervals, a storm lantern cast a fitful glow over the dripping bags.

Crouching down, they moved forward, Maitland in the lead. It was only half a mile back to Knightsbridge, and luckily the tunnel was unbreached at any other point. A few people lay about in makeshift sleeping bags by the storm lights – claustrophobes, Maitland assumed, who were more terrified of their basements and the Underground than of the wind, and who preferred the surface tunnels with their long corridors and spaced lights. Tripping over abandoned clothing and cooking utensils, they reached the station in five minutes. The entranceway had been heavily fortified with reinforced concrete by the army. Two armed policemen in black wind suits checked their passes, then directed them to the signals unit set up in the ticket booth.

After the deserted, darkened streets, the station was a blaze of lights, packed with thousands of people huddled about on the upper level with their bundles of luggage, walling off crude cubicles with blankets and raincoats, cooking over primus stoves, queueing endlessly at the latrines. Sleeping figures and parcels of luggage crowded the floor. They picked their way over the outstretched limbs, trying not to disturb the fretfully sleeping children and older people, till they located the two signallers operating the radio transmitter.

After five minutes they contacted the Hammersmith control point and confirmed the driver's arrangement that a carrier from Brandon Hall would pick them up in a couple of hours' time.

People were sitting all the way down the stationary escalators, huddled against each other's knees, blankets wrapped around them, plastic bags at their feet containing gnawed loaves of bread, a few meagre cans and battered thermoses. Stepping past them, Maitland's group made their way down to the lower platforms, where some semblance of order had been enforced. Women and children had been allocated the westbound platform, while the men and service units occupied the eastbound. Wooden partitions had been erected and police patrolled the exits and entrances.

They were steered onto the platform, jumped down between the rails and began to walk along to the next station, South Kensington. Electric bulbs strung along the tunnel shone down onto the track. On the platform above them a throng of soldiers and other men lay in their sleeping packs, most of them asleep, a few watching impassively, their eyes dull.

They had nearly reached the end of the platform when someone ahead sat up and waved to Maitland. He turned around, recognized the hall porter from the apartment block.

'Dr Maitland! Spare a minute, will you, Doctor?'

He was sitting back against a large expensive suitcase to which Maitland guessed he had helped himself in one of the deserted apartments.

'Doctor, I wanted to tell you. Mrs Maitland's still up there.'

Maitland stiffened. 'What? Are you sure?' When the

porter nodded, he clenched his fists involuntarily. He had over-estimated Susan's resourcefulness. 'Crazy fool! Couldn't you make her come down here?'

'I told her, Doctor, believe me. She was there only yesterday. Said she wanted to stay and watch the houses falling.'

'*Watch* them? Where is she? In the basement?'

The porter shook his head. 'Up in your flat, Doctor. The windows are all smashed and she's living in the lift now. It's stuck on the sixth floor.'

Maitland hesitated, looking over his shoulder. His two companions were just disappearing around the first bend in the tunnel. They would reach Hammersmith in forty-five minutes, probably have more than an hour to wait before Brandon Hall got around to picking them up.

'Can I still get to Lowndes Square?' he asked the porter. 'The tunnels are standing?'

The porter nodded. 'Follow the one down Sloane Street, then cut through the Pakistan Embassy garage. Takes you straight into the block. Watch it though, Doctor. There's big stuff coming down all the time.'

Maitland jumped onto the platform and retraced his steps up the escalator. He reached the entranceway and pressed through the late arrivals pushing in from the tunnel, even less well equipped than those already there. Many of them were without bedding or food, holding a milk bottle full of water as their sole rations for the next few weeks. Maitland checked each one of them carefully in case Susan had decided to take shelter, then crouched down and entered the tunnel.

Crude signposts had been put up at junction points within the tunnel system. Turning right into Sloane Street, he ran with his head down, feeling his way along the irregular corridor of bursting sandbags. A few cracks of light added to the scanty illumination provided by the storm lanterns. Gusts of air poured in, spuming white cement dust like escape valves blowing off steam.

Two hundred yards down Sloane Street the tunnel ended in a short flight of steps into a small fortified basement below one of the office blocks. This had recently been used as a temporary first-aid post. Two or three cubicles stood against one wall, behind a boiler. There was a tin desk littered with forms and empty dried-milk cartons.

Crossing the basement, he kicked back a door into the garbage-disposal unit and climbed another staircase into a fortified passageway, where pit props were placed at two-yard intervals. This branched left and right when it reached Lowndes Square. The left-hand section ended abruptly in a heap of rubble where one of the older houses had collapsed into the road. The other ran in the direction of the apartment house, and Maitland climbed through a breach in the wall into the basement garage of the Pakistan Embassy.

In the ramp outside, a long black Cadillac limousine sagged back on a broken rear axle, tyres flat, windows shattered, a collection of half-packed suitcases abandoned by the open trunk. Protecting his face from the stones and tiles ricocheting between the high walls, Maitland dived through into the service doorway of the apartment house.

All the apartments had been abandoned, and air whirled around the stairway, changing its direction every few seconds, driving clouds of dust and rubble up and down the steps.

Maitland pulled himself up to the sixth floor and looked into the elevator. A small leather armchair stood inside it, two dirty cushions and a screwed-up blanket revealing the outline of some small figure.

Maitland raced up the next three floors to his own apartment, pushed back the door. The hall was in darkness; air swirled through from the lounge, dragging at the litter of old newspapers and magazines. He ran through, steadying himself as he reached the door. The French windows had been torn out and the steel frames quivered as the wind rushed past the end of the building, an enormous turbulent vortex bursting explosively around the ragged stonework. The outside balcony had been ripped off and all the furniture in the room had been sucked out by the vortex and carried away over the roof of the Embassy below.

For a moment he felt that he was standing over the propellors of some gigantic aircraft carrier, gazing out at the writhing wake as the vessel plunged through boiling seas, shielded from the sky by the overhanging flight deck. He was looking westward across the city, the storm-driven rooftops stretching to the horizon like huge ragged waves, obscured by a spray of dust and grit.

'Quite a view, isn't it, Donald?' he heard someone say quietly at his shoulder. He turned to see Susan in the doorway behind him.

'Susan! What are you doing here?' He reached out to her. 'Get your things together and come down to the Underground Station. Everyone's sheltering there.'

Susan shook her head and stepped past him into the lounge, swaying as the wind caught her. Her hair clung in a matted net around her face, grey with dust and dirt. She still wore the cocktail dress he had last seen her in. The full skirt was torn and stained, the net underskirt trailing at her heels. One of the shoulder straps had gone and the front of the dress hung down loosely, revealing her scratched dirty skin.

He caught her as she rode a gust of air that swept out through the balcony, pulled her against himself.

'Susan, for God's sake, what are you playing at? This is no time for putting on an act.'

She leaned against him, smiling wanly. 'I'm not, Donald,' she said mildly, 'believe me. I just like to watch the wind. The whole of London's starting to fall down. Soon it'll all be blown away, Peter and you and everybody.'

She looked tired and hungry. Maitland wondered whether she had eaten. Perhaps the porter had bartered a little food for a decanter of whisky, tried to keep her going.

Maitland put his arm around her shoulders, began to draw her into the corridor. 'Come on, darling. This whole building will be coming down too in a few hours. You've got to get out of here. The Underground's the only place.'

She twisted away from him, revealing a sudden unexpected strength.

'Not for me, Donald,' she said evenly, stepping backward into the lounge. 'You go, if you want to. I'm staying here.' When he reached out to her again she stepped back quickly, only nine or ten feet from the inferno raging outside the balcony, and poised there, her hair swept back off her head.

When he hesitated, she glanced at him pityingly for a moment, then turned and looked over the rooftops. 'I've been frightened for too long, Donald. Of Daddy, and you and myself. Now I'm not any longer. You go and dig a hole in the ground somewhere if you want to –'

Her eyes were away from him and Maitland dived forward and seized her arm. Clenching her teeth, she kicked out at him, her slim body uncoiling like a frantic spring. They struggled silently, then Susan wrenched away and stepped back.

'Susan!' Maitland shouted at her. For a moment she stared wildly at him, then moved away. She was only a few feet from the open window. Suddenly the wind caught her. Before he could move it whirled her back off her feet against the door frame; then spun her head over heels into the open air.

Down on his knees, Maitland saw her for an instant, catapulted through the updraught rising from the street, bounce off the roof of the Embassy building and then spin away like a smashed doll into the maze of rooftops beyond. A few feet from him the air pounded at the door frame, ripping away the masonry from the exposed edge.

For five minutes he lay on the floor, head pressed to the dull parquet, the pain and violence of Susan's death stunning his mind. Then, slowly, he pulled himself backward to the door and got to his feet.

The strength of the wind had increased significantly as he retraced his steps through the Pakistan Embassy and along the tunnel to the first-aid post. Somewhere the system of emergency tunnels had been badly breached. As he stepped through the aid post something struck the ceiling above his head, splitting the concrete and sending down a shower of dust. The building began to quiver restlessly, indicating that the roof had been breached. Soon heavy sections of masonry would come toppling through the floors, knock out the central transverse supports and allow the wind to push the walls in like cardboard hoardings.

Maitland climbed into the Sloane Street tunnel. A hundred yards away a single lamp flickered dismally, illuminating the narrow corridor of leaking sandbags, the moisture exuded from the wet cement making it resemble an abandoned sewer. Head down, he hurried along to the station entrance.

He ran down the steps, then pitched forward on his knees, banging his head against the far wall. Picking up his torch, he shone it around the floor, feeling for the steps with his hands.

Half-way down the staircase, heavy steel shutters had been sealed into place, an immovable lid of three-inch plate that cut him off from the sanctuary below.

Trying not to lose his self-control, he climbed out of the staircase and re-entered the tunnel. He switched the torch off to conserve the battery and groped along the walls, his only hope to get out of the tunnel before it collapsed and find a deep basement in one of the buildings off the street that would remain intact when its upper floors gave way.

Above him, apparently far away to the left, a dim rumbling had started. He stopped and waited as it grew nearer, flicking on the torch. Then, ten yards away, in a cataract of dust and noise, an enormous section of masonry plunged straight through the roof of the tunnel, letting in a tornado of exploding brickwork that drove Maitland backward off his feet. As he pulled himself upright the entire roof of the tunnel bulged inward, then collapsed in a vast avalanche of debris that poured in around him, shutting out the light that had burst through the first aperture.

Maitland stumbled back, shielding his head from the falling rubble. Massive tremors struck the walls of the tunnel, and its floor began to tilt in awkward jerks.

Maitland waited, ready to retreat back into the entrance-way, watching the dust swirl around him in the thin beam of the torch. After a few minutes he edged forward carefully. The quake had ended, the building that had collapsed across the tunnel – Harvey Nichols, one of the big department stores – had settled itself.

A few yards ahead the tunnel ended abruptly. An entire floor section had sliced through it like a guillotine, sealing it off as cleanly and absolutely as the bulkhead ten yards behind him. Maitland started to kick away the debris around the slab, then gave up and backed away from the acrid dust.

He was trapped neatly, like a rat in a pain corridor, except that here there would be no further signals. He had a runway about ten feet long, bounded at either end by impassable walls. Disturbed for half a minute, the air quickly settled, soon was completely still.

Suddenly he felt weak, and dropped to his knees. Putting his hand up to his head, he felt blood eddying from a wide wound across the back of his scalp. He sat down and started to take out his first-aid kit, then realized he was losing consciousness. He managed to switch off the torch just as his mind began to spin and fall, plunging through the surface of a deep inky well.

Around him, the rubble began to shift again.

By now the pyramid was almost complete. Its apex over-topped the steel windshields, and a subsidiary line of shields, staked to the upper slopes of the pyramid, protected the men scaling the peak. They moved slowly, strung together by long cables, forming the last cornices and lynchstones, dragged and buffeted together like blind slaves.

Below, most of the huge graders and mixers had turned away, were laying and forming the long ramparts which led into the wind from the base of the pyramid. Ten feet thick and twice as high at their deepest point, they rose from the black earth, stretching from the body of the pyramid like the recumbent forelimbs of some headless sphinx.

Watching them from his eyrie in the pyramid, the iron-faced man christened the ramparts in his mind, calling them the gateways of the whirlwind.

Chapter 5

The Scavengers

'Pat.'

The girl stirred, murmured something as she lay half asleep in his arms on the old mattress against the wall, then nestled closer to him.

With his free hand Lanyon stroked her blonde hair, sweeping it back gently over her small neat ears, then kissed her carefully on the forehead, trying to keep his four-day stubble away from her skin. Pressed against him, she felt warm and comfortable, wearing his leather jacket around her shoulders while her own coat covered their legs, buttoned up around them.

Lanyon looked down and watched her face, her eyelids moving occasionally as she reached towards the surface of consciousness, her full lips slightly parted in a relaxed smile, wide smooth cheekbones still unblemished by the duststorms. She breathed steadily, then slowly raised her head and slipped his left arm from beneath it.

'Steve?' She stirred, opened her eyes sleepily as he disengaged his legs from the coat.

He bent down and kissed her mouth gently. 'It's O.K., darling. You sleep. I'm just going to smell the air.'

He covered her carefully, then stood up and stepped across her to the other end of the pillbox, head stooped to avoid the roof. Outside, the air whistled past interminably, the turbulence around the hill face making it difficult to assess its velocity.

Lanyon searched his pockets, found a packet of Caporals he had discovered in a cupboard at the airfield, lit one carefully and went over to the gun slit. They had blocked it with a heap of bricks and stones. Pulling a few of them away, Lanyon carefully dislodged a brick in the centre of the pile and slowly slid it back.

From his watch he noted it was 7.35 a.m. Outside, through his narrow gun slit, he could see across the ruined dam down the valley to Genoa and the sea. Clouds of dust and vapour lowered the ceiling to little more than two or three hundred yards, and visibility to half a mile.

The pillbox had been built into the mouth of one of the caves in the cliff face overlooking the east side of the dam. Shielded by the 300-foot bluff above and recessed ten feet back into the cave mouth, it provided an excellent vantage point from which to survey the valley below. Lanyon noticed that the dam had almost completely vanished by now, a thin ragged rim of concrete four or five feet high all that remained of the original 100-foot wall. The reservoir behind it had been drained, the bed eaten smooth by the air passing overhead, strewn now with countless boulders and rock fragments blown in from the hills.

Lanyon wondered if most of the world's great rivers had been similarly drained. Was the Amazon a dry mile-wide ribbon of sand, the Mississippi a 2,000-mile-long inland beach?

Three miles away the coastline and the sea were a blur, but the port of Genoa appeared to be sealed by a ring of wrecks. Almost certainly the *Terrapin* would still be at its berth in the sub-pen, unless he had been abandoned and the ship recruited for some other special mission, in which case it was probably lying on the bottom of the ocean. The chances of reaching the sub-pens seemed slim, but over the past days they had managed to get from the airfield to their present retreat, and with luck they would keep moving.

Lanyon pulled on the cigarette, watching a large wooden shed sail through the air fifty feet off the ground about half a mile away. It was still intact, rotating slowly, apparently just dislodged from some protected site. Suddenly it struck the shoulder of one of the hills leaning into the valley, and immediately disintegrated like a bursting shell into a momentary cloud of pieces each no bigger than a matchbox.

He replaced the brick and packed the wind slit carefully. Patricia was still asleep, apparently exhausted. They had arrived at the pillbox two days ago, after a frantic ninety-mile-an-hour ride in a renovated staff car. Here they had enough food for a few more days – two or three cans of salt pork they had found in the basement, a basket of rotting peaches and half a dozen bottles of coarse wine.

Lanyon slipped out through the doorway into the rear of the cave. Ten yards from the pillbox the floor dipped downward and expanded into a wide gallery which had been used as a mess room by the troops guarding the dam. Tiers of bunks lined the walls, and two long rough tables were in the centre, strewn with unwashed cutlery and bits of bread. Water dripped from a score of cracks in the ceiling, forming in pools on the floor or running away into the other caves leading off from the gallery.

Lanyon picked up a clean jerrican, scooped up some of the water and then put it on the table. Treading through the debris of sodden magazines and cigarette packets, he made his way to the rear of the gallery, took one of the lower passageways that had been fitted with a simple railing. It curved downward slightly, and appeared to be the emergency exit out into the ravine behind the cliff. A side road had led into the ravine, but Lanyon had been unable to steer the car into it when they arrived, and they had been carried into the lee of the cliff and left to crawl out of the wreck and climb up the face to the pillbox fifty feet above.

At several points the cave broke through the side of the cliff and through the apertures Lanyon could see across to the sheer brownstone face twenty yards away. Air gusted into the ravine, but small firs and thornbushes still clung to rocky ledges. He and Patricia would probably be able to use the route if it led in the right direction.

He stepped out of the mouth at the bottom and looked around him. The cliffs on either side went up 300 feet and a continuous cascade of stones and rocks fell from their tops, spitting at the ground around Lanyon's feet. Bracing himself against the wall of the ravine, he slid along through the down-draught of air, trying to see where the narrow corridor led. Overhanging shelves of rock shielded him occasionally from the hail. The high gulleys ran away at oblique angles into the hills, and the whole system appeared to move southwest, in the direction of Genoa and the sea.

One hundred yards out, he turned back and re-entered the cave.

Patricia was sitting up when he reached the pillbox, combing her hair in the mirror of her compact. She had lost her handbag and make-up but her lips were full and red, her skin a honey cream, and she looked fresh and vital, even though she had been through the last five days with little to eat and a minimum of rest.

'Hello, Steve.' She smiled up at him. 'Anything happening?'

'Still blowing hard,' he told her. 'Looks as if it's nearing the two hundred-mile-an-hour mark. How do you feel?'

'Wonderful. This is the life that really does a girl good.' She reached out to take his hand, the lapels of the windbreaker swinging back.

'Whoops,' she said. She pulled Lanyon down to her. 'Anyone else around?' she asked.

Lanyon shook his head, grinned affectionately at her.

'No. Go ahead, though, I'm watching.'

Patricia put her finger on his nose, pushed him back. 'Now, now, Commander, just put away that naughty periscope. *And* you haven't shaved.'

Lanyon took her in his arms and they wrestled playfully on the mattress. He kissed her hard on the mouth, then sat up and looked at his watch. 'Pat, I hate to break up a party, but if we're going to get out of here we'd better start moving soon. Do you feel strong enough?'

Lying back, she nodded and put her hand on his arm.

'Just about. What do we have to do?'

'There's a ravine that leads off towards the city. With luck we may be able to reach the outskirts, then pick up some military transport.' He looked at his watch. 'I'm frightened that if we don't get back soon Matheson may accidentally scuttle the ship. Or else that it'll be detailed off on some other wild-goose chase.'

He stood up and pulled a can out of the Italian army haversack hung below the gun slit. Clipping open the lid, he carried it and the jerrican across to Patricia.

'It's probably worth trying to eat some more of this stuff, even though it doesn't look it. Anyway, if it's any consolation it's not much worse than the chow aboard the *Terrapin*.'

Forking some of the pork into her mouth, Patricia pulled a face. 'Crumbs, I don't know whether I'll come with you after all.' She paused, her face worried. 'Steve, do you really think they'll let me on? I know you're the captain and all that, but after the admirals' wives have made themselves comfortable there just may not be enough room for a working gal from NBC.'

Lanyon smiled at her. 'Relax. There aren't any admirals' wives in the neighbourhood, let alone any admirals. You'll be on board even if I have to marry you.'

'*Even?*' Patricia said in a playful tone. 'Well, thanks.'

A vortex of air whirling down the face of the cliff pulled at the pillbox, shifting the stones heaped into the window slit, spitting dust over their heads. Lanyon took her hand and steadied her, then lifted her to her feet. His hands felt her shoulders under the windbreaker, her ash-blonde hair billowing across his face as her head tipped back under the pressure of his mouth on her lips.

Entering the ravine, they moved cautiously along the east wall, sheltering under the overhanging shelves while showers of stones drove down from the roof, darting forward during the clear periods. Air swirled around them, exploding with vicious snaps as vortices span off the lips of the ravine and burst against the floor 300 feet below. Higher up, just under the roof, they could see a few forlorn firs clinging to their footholds in the sides of the rock face, their outlines blurring as they quivered in the dust-storm.

They reached the point to which Lanyon had explored previously, where the ravine divided, the larger space, on the northern side, gradually opening out into a wide-walled valley, across which the air stream moved like a huge wave front over a rockpool, sucking away every loose fragment of rock, every vestige of vegetation. Lanyon realized that if they ventured into the valley the negative-pressure field would probably suck them straight up into the air and whirl them away towards the hills in the west.

The southern division was little more than a narrow fissure in the rock face, shelving away towards the southeast at a gradually tilting angle. Once a small stream had splashed down it, and the stones were smooth and polished, still damp in the sandy bed.

They climbed along it, a narrow ribbon of daylight winding somewhere above them to the left. Lanyon held Patricia's hand, steered her over heavy boulders and spurs, pulling her across smooth polished slabs that fell across their pathway like eroded tombstones.

For half an hour they made steady progress eastward, moving, Lanyon estimated, at least a mile nearer the city, almost in sight of the farthest suburbs. The ravine opened into a narrow flat-bottomed canyon, the sheer face on its eastern side sheltering the tree-covered slopes stretching away from them.

Patricia pulled Lanyon's arm.

'Steve, look. Over there. Is that a farmhouse?'

Lanyon followed her pointing finger, saw the low ragged outline of what had once been a castellated wall curving away along a road which crossed the end of the canyon.

'May be part of an old castle or chateau,' Lanyon commented. 'With luck we'll find someone else there. Come on.'

On their right the ground shelved steeply to the crest of the cliff 150 feet above them. Built onto the supporting shoulders was what had once been a monastery, a long two-storeyed complex of massive stone walls and buttresses five or six hundred years old. The top story and roof had been stripped away but the lower section, just under the crest, was still intact, rooted into the sloping rock face below.

The ruined wall enclosed what was left of the garden and vineyards. Half-way along, an arched doorway let into a yard between low outbuildings. Lanyon took Patricia's arm, and they bent down and moved slowly along the wall towards the entrance. They paused in one of the doorways, and Lanyon pounded on the heavy wooden shutters.

'No one here!' he yelled to Patricia. 'Let's see if we can get inside.' They moved around the yard, trying the windows and shutters. All the entrances had been carefully sealed, the doors into the main building braced with padlocked crossbars. Lanyon pointed to the circular stone lid of the grain shute recessed into the cobbles.

'There's a good chance we'll be able to get in through here.' He pulled out his jack knife, snapped the blade open and pried it in under the lip of the lid, tearing his nails as he wrestled the heavy disc out of its socket. Finally he freed it, dragged it to one side and peered down into the shute. Fifteen feet below the polished metal slide angled down into one of the storage silos, wooden stalls half filled with grain. Lanyon took Patricia's hands, watched her disappear down into the dim half light.

He followed her quickly, trying to brace himself but ending up to his waist in the soft rustling grain. They shook their clothes free, Patricia leaning on Lanyon's shoulder, and moved below the arched ceiling towards a low flight of steps that led into another storeroom. Here and there light filtered in through narrow grilles, revealing the dim outlines of corridors winding between massive pillars and vaulted ceilings.

The next storeroom was empty. They crossed it, walked down a short flight of ancient steps into the basement of the monastery itself.

'Looks as if this monastery's been disused for some while,' Lanyon commented to Patricia. 'The local farmers probably work the land and store their grain here.'

They reached heavy wooden doors at the end of the corridor. Lanyon turned the circular hasp in the lock and peered through into total darkness. Taking out his flashlight, he flashed it on, then whistled sharply.

'Wait a minute, Pat. I think I'm wrong.'

They were looking into a large storeroom about thirty yards long, floor and far wall cut into the cliff itself, roof carried by massive buttresses. Stacked in lines down the full length of the room were hundreds of huge crates and cartons, their contents glinting in the torch beam.

'The monks must have stored everything away here before they left,' Lanyon muttered. They moved forward down one of the aisles. He brushed against a square waist-high object that gonged metallically, then shone the torch on a large white washing machine.

He tapped it to attract Patricia's attention. 'Up to date, aren't they?' Moving the torch, he then saw that there were half a dozen other machines next to it, all of them taped with the manufacturer's protective wrappers.

Pausing, he started to examine the stacks of cases more carefully.

'These haven't even been used,' Patricia commented.

Lanyon nodded. 'I know. Something curious about all this. Look at those.' He swung the flashlight against the wall, where the blank eyes of twenty or thirty TV receivers stared back at them, like a display in a darkened shop window. Next to the TV sets were two big red-and-yellow plastic-fronted jukeboxes, and beyond these a pile of radios, vacuum cleaners and electric stoves, heaped with smaller cartons containing irons, hair driers and other domestic appliances.

Flashing the torch, Lanyon walked slowly down the aisle. On the left, down the centre of the storeroom, was a solid wall of what appeared to be machine tools – lathes, circular saws, jig-cutting equipment – the steel bearings and drives pasted over with brown tape.

'One of the stores must be using this place as its warehouse,' Patricia remarked. 'Strange selection of items, though.'

Lanyon nodded. 'How did they get all this stuff up here?' They had reached the far end of the room, and he turned the handle of the double oak doors. 'Looks to me –'

As he opened the door, lights moved at the far end of the corridor beyond, and he had a brief impression of four or five men shifting some bulky object on a small trolley. He pushed the door to and snapped off the torch, just as a shout of recognition went up.

'Steve, they've seen us!' Lanyon held Patricia's arm.

'Listen, Pat, I'm not sure who these people are. They look like looters to me. We'd better get out of here.'

He switched on the torch again and they ran quickly down the aisle past the stacks of radios and washing machines. As they reached the doorway Lanyon saw a large black-garbed figure moving silently below the vaulted arches of the adjacent storeroom. The man noticed the beam of Lanyon's torch and immediately slid back into the darkness behind one of the pillars.

Lanyon pulled Patricia back into an alcove between the door and the stack of TV sets. He slipped his .45 automatic out of its holster, eased up the safety catch.

'Wait here, Pat,' he whispered. 'Try not to move. Someone came in after us through the grain store. I'll see if I can get behind him.' He felt her hand hold his tightly, her face tense. He dived through the doorway and crouched down behind one of the pillars, just as the doors on the far side of the storeroom swung back and torches flared across the piles of merchandise.

Lanyon began to edge forward to a central pillar that fanned out in the middle of the chamber. Ahead of him he could hear someone moving along the stonework.

He was half-way across when lights flooded on in the storeroom behind him, a string of bulbs around the walls filling the chamber with hard white light. Voices shouted out again, feet hammered across the stone floor.

Spinning around, he ran back to the storeroom, reached the door just as Patricia, hiding in the alcove a few feet from him, screamed.

Dazzled for a moment by the light, Lanyon's eyes raced around the room. He caught a fleeting glimpse of two swarthy-faced men in black trousers and windbreakers swarming between the crates, then saw a third moving nimbly half-way down the aisle, a heavy Mauser in one hand, the long barrel pointed at Patricia.

The shot roared out into the confined air, slamming against the tiers of metal cabinets, the flame flashing off the TV screens. One next to Patricia shattered in a burst of glass. The man with the Mauser stopped, feet placed wide apart, then raised the gun again.

Dropping to one knee, Lanyon straightened his arm, steadied his elbow with his left hand, then fired quickly. The power of the .45 stunned the air for a moment, and the two men on the far side of the room ducked down. The gunman with the Mauser had been kicked back onto the floor by the heavy bullet passing through his chest, and lay inertly on his face, blood leaking slowly across the cobbles.

Lanyon knelt down to see if Patricia was all right, but out of the side of his eye was aware of someone bending over him. He managed to duck just as the blow caught his ear, rode onto the floor with it. As he started to get up the man kicked him viciously in the chest and Lanyon staggered back, ribs tearing with pain, trying to level his automatic.

Then the other two men were on him, wrestling him down onto the floor again, their fists slamming at his face. A heavy boot stamped onto his hand, knocking the gun away, and then he was pulled back on his feet and propped up against one of the packing cases. He had a confused image of Patricia down on her knees; then a big man with a red vicious face clubbed him savagely across the forehead with the barrel of the .45. Lanyon sagged over and smashed on the floor. The big man snapped the gun butt into his hand and levelled it at Lanyon, his eyes narrowing like an insane pig's.

The two other men stood waiting expectantly, one of them with his knee in the small of Patricia's back, holding her down on the floor. Lanyon rolled wearily against the case, trying to clear his eyes of the blood running from the wound across his temple, barely aware of the gun barrel a few inches from his head.

Suddenly the big man paused, lowered the gun, then stepped forward and ripped open Lanyon's windbreaker, grabbing the lapels of his drill jacket, fingering the gold USN tabs. He stuffed the automatic into his belt and cuffed Lanyon's head back, running his strong thick fingers over Lanyon's bruised cheeks.

He tapped Lanyon's face softly, and a grim smile broke across his huge features. He took Lanyon by the shoulders, shook him twice in his strong arms.

'Eh, Capitano!' he called out. 'You O.K., boy?'

When Lanyon steadied himself and looked at him, he stepped back and gestured to his men to help Patricia to her feet. Then he grinned at Lanyon, pulled one of the men over to him by the shoulder, and spoke to him rapidly in Italian, jerking his thumb at Lanyon.

The man nodded, then spoke to Lanyon.

'You help Luigi at Viamillia,' he told Lanyon matter-of-factly. 'He ask how you feeling?'

Lanyon looked across at Luigi, massaging his painful neck with one hand. Dimly he remembered the huge distraught Italian in the damaged church, hurling the debris off the pews like a maddened bull.

Patricia stumbled across to him and he put his arm around her, pressed her head into his shoulder.

'Steve, are you all right?' she gasped. 'Who are they? What are they going to do with us?'

Lanyon pulled himself together, managed to smile back at Luigi. He spoke to the interpreter, a small thin-faced man with a striped shirt.

'Sure, I remember him. Tell him I'm just about in one piece, but I could use some water.' While the thin-faced man interpreted, Lanyon patted Patricia's shoulder. 'We ran into him in a small town on the way out of Genoa. His family were trapped in a church. We helped get them out.'

Luigi nodded to the interpreter, gestured them all across the storeroom to the door. Slowly they made their way out, avoiding the body of the gunman lying on the floor in a widening pool of blood. Luigi picked up the Mauser, rammed it into his belt next to Lanyon's .45. They entered the corridor, then turned off through a small doorway into a narrow low-ceilinged room where a single light burned low over a bare wooden table. Inset into the walls were four bunks, the bedding rumpled and filthy.

One of the men snapped off the corridor lights and closed the door behind them, but Lanyon noticed a small printing press on the trolley outside.

Luigi pulled up a chair by the table and Lanyon lowered himself slowly into it, Patricia sitting down on the edge of the bed behind him. Luigi barked at the two men; one slipped outside and returned a moment later with a jug full of water, and the little interpreter rooted along the shelf over the fireplace and produced a grimy glass. Luigi took

102

it, pulled the cork out of a bottle of Chianti, poured some into the glass and passed it across to Patricia, then pushed the bottle over to Lanyon.

Lanyon swabbed down his face and neck, then tore one pocket off his shirt and pasted it over the wound on his forehead. Slightly refreshed, he sat back and put his hand reassuringly on Patricia's knee, squeezed her thigh.

First tipping the neck of the bottle towards Luigi, he filled his mouth with the harsh bitter wine, then passed it back across the table.

Luigi pulled up a chair and sat down. He jerked a thumb over his shoulder. 'Ship? You?' He spoke to the interpreter, who was clearing away the jug of water.

'Luigi asks if you go back for your ship?'

Lanyon nodded. 'Trying to. How can we get there – the submarine base? You know any covered roads?'

The interpreter translated this for Luigi, and the two men looked at each other silently for a moment. Then Luigi frowned and muttered something.

'Very strong wind,' the interpreter explained. 'Can't move on the streets now. Big hotels, houses –' he snapped his fingers '– all going bang!'

Lanyon glanced at his watch. It was 2.35. Soon it would be dark; movement would be impossible until the next morning.

'What about everything in the storeroom?' he asked curtly. 'How did you get it up here? You were carrying something big in just now.'

There was a lengthy consultation, during which the interpreter shrugged repeatedly and Luigi appeared to be trying to make up his mind.

Lanyon spoke to Patricia over his shoulder. 'They must be looting the warehouses and stores around here. Presumably looting is now punishable by death. I suppose he's afraid we'll report him to the military governor.'

The other man, older, with a dry wizened face and a

cropped skull, joined in the conversation, throwing sharp reminders across the table at Luigi, who was fingering his gun belt uneasily. Finally he appeared to come to a decision. He rapped something out and they all fell silent.

Luigi smiled slowly at Lanyon, relaxing perceptibly, then leaned forward and pulled a crumpled bundle of paper out of his hip pocket. Carefully his big workman's fingers pried the pages open, and he spread out a battered map of the city, streets ringed crudely with pencilled circles, marked into a series of zones.

The interpreter pulled up a chair and pointed to the map. 'We take you,' he said to Lanyon after he and Luigi had muttered softly to each other. 'But, er, you know –' he made a gesture around the eyes, placing the tips of his fingers together over the bridge of his nose.

'Blindfold?' Lanyon suggested.

'*Si*, blindfold.' The interpreter smiled, then elaborated slowly. 'And blindfold afterward, you understand? All blindfold.'

Lanyon nodded. Luigi was watching narrowly, sizing him up.

'Looks as if they're happy,' Lanyon said to Patricia.

'How can they take us, though?' she asked.

Lanyon shrugged. 'Cellars, basements, underground tunnels. An old city like Genoa must be honeycombed with secret passageways. I suppose this monastery had one down to the city for the benefit of the monks on Saturday night in the bad old days. They've been moving some pretty big stuff in so I should think we're in luck. The only problem is how to get into the base itself once we reach the downtown section of the city. We'll just have to pray we'll be able to pick up transport somewhere. There isn't a hope of our covering even five yards out in the open on our own.'

He watched the big Italian tracing a route on the map, then spoke to the interpreter.

'Tell me, is his wife O.K.? She was in the church.'

When the interpreter nodded, he added: 'Tell Luigi I'm sorry about the shooting in here.'

The interpreter grinned, began to chuckle to himself. 'That's O.K.' he said. 'More for us, eh?'

Single file, Luigi leading with the interpreter, followed by Lanyon and Patricia, the third man in the rear, they entered the passageway running down from the monastery.

This had been cut straight through the soft chalk of the cliff, and ran for about a mile, linking together three churches with the monastery. Six feet high and about a yard across, it was just enough for the trolley, but the effort of moving it uphill must have been enormous. How far below the surface they were Lanyon found it difficult to estimate. They emerged into the crypt of the nearest church and for the first time could hear the wind drumming past overhead, its deep all-pervading whine singing through the angles in the shattered ruins. Then the tunnel sank below ground again and the sounds were lost.

Gradually Lanyon noticed that the air had begun to come to life in the passageway. Odd shifts of wind edged past, periodically sudden gusts of grit bellowed into their faces, and Luigi would stop and switch off his torch. However, it was obvious he was more afraid of the military authorities than of the wind.

'What speed is it now?' Lanyon asked the interpreter as they crouched down during one of the pauses, waiting for Luigi to return from reconnoitring ahead.

'Three hundred kilometres,' the man replied. 'Maybe more.'

Lanyon jerked a finger upward. 'What about Genoa? People all right?'

The interpreter laughed shortly. He spread his hands out sideways in a quick movement. 'All phht,' he said, 'Gone with the wind. Everything blown down. Luigi save

105

things – radios, jukeboxes, you know, TVs. All for to-morrow.'

Lanyon smiled to himself at the man's naïveté and super-optimism in assuming that when the wind subsided their stock of TV sets and washing machines would make easily negotiable currency. About the only thing that would be of any immediate use was the printing press. After this holo-caust the reassembling bureaucracies of the world would have their presses working night and day churning out paper to fill the vacuum left by the wind.

The second church had collapsed into its crypt and a detour supported by small girders had been driven through the piles of masonry. Now the wind filled the tunnel, blow-ing straight through at a steady ten or fifteen miles per hour. They had reached the midtown section of the city and the passageway took advantage of the old city wall, running along beside it for half a mile as it curved down into the centre of modern Genoa towards the harbour. The floor was slick with moisture and twice he and Patricia slipped onto their hands.

The passageway opened out into the middle of a maze of tomblike vaults, abandoned wine cellars somewhere off the main square. Ancient stairways, deep dips worn down their centres, spiralled away to upper galleries. Luigi pulled out his map and he and the interpreter began to confer, pointing in various directions around them.

Lanyon went over to them. He indicated the vaulted ceil-ing, and said: 'Why don't we get up to the street, see if we can spot a military transport?'

Luigi shook his head slowly with a grim smile, and spoke to the interpreter, who took Lanyon's arm and led him up a ramp to the gallery above. They climbed a further staircase, leaving Patricia and two men in a small circle of light far below, then moved along a ledge across the massive blocks of the city wall. Ahead of them was a foot-wide arrow slit. The interpreter gestured Lanyon over to it and he craned up and saw that a thick piece of perspex had been fitted into the hole, affording a view over the entire city.

Directly below were the ragged remains of some building which had collapsed, exposing this section of the city wall. The rectangular outlines of the foundations suggested that it had been a multi-storeyed office block, but almost nothing of it was left.

Beyond it Genoa stretched towards the sea a mile away.

To Lanyon it appeared to be undergoing a massive artillery bombardment. On all sides the remains of houses and shops were collapsing, exploding in clouds of debris and rubble that vanished in a few seconds, swept out towards the sea on the endless conveyor of the air stream. The scene reminded Lanyon of World War II Berlin, a vast desert of gutted ruins, isolated walls that ran up five or six storeys, buildings stripped to their steel superstructures, streets that had vanished under the piles of masonry, leaving a dead land as shapeless and amorphous as a slag heap.

To the south-west, half a mile away, an enormous blur of spray hung over the port area, for once obscuring the ceiling of red-brown dust that had covered them for the last week. Lanyon could just make out the square roofs of the naval base, revealed now that the intervening buildings had come down, but the pens themselves were too low to be visible.

The interpreter called to him, and left the window and made his way down to the others below. Suddenly Lanyon began to doubt whether they could possibly reach the pens. It was plain that no surface transport was moving around and the tunnels would never extend as far as the dock area, let alone below the boundary of the base.

Patricia was watching him anxiously and he gave her an encouraging smile. Together they moved after Luigi as he climbed down a narrow spiral stairway that led off one of the side tunnels. Here the stonework was of more recent origin. The steps were less worn, and a hand rail of extruded piping had been fitted. Lanyon was wondering where the stairway led when Luigi reached a door at the bottom and wrenched it back.

Immediately a gust of foul air drove up into their faces.

They had entered the sewers. Hands shielding their mouths, they stepped out of the stairway into a narrow stone landing that overlooked the sewer, a long cavern fifteen feet in diameter that wound away from them. It had almost run dry, but a narrow stream of fluid a few inches deep trickled along the bottom of the course, its surface rippled by the air driving across it.

Flashing his torch, Luigi examined the roof and the arching semicircle of damp brickwork, dented here and there by the impact of the buildings collapsing above. They began to move along the ledge. A hundred yards ahead they crossed a small bridge that took them through a narrow archway into a parallel sewer, which divided and curved westward towards the harbour. Smaller branch sewers joined it, but most of the way they were able to stay on the ledge, only twice having to get down into the course itself to surmount an obstruction.

The sewer was widening almost to the size of a subway tunnel. Trying to guess where they were being led, Lanyon suddenly noticed a second odour, sharp and tangy, overlaying that of the sewer. Brine! They were nearing the sea. Then he remembered that, as he berthed the *Terrapin,* he had seen the vents of half a dozen sewer pipes just below the harbour wall some two hundred yards from the sub-pens. A long concrete breakwater, topped with double wave barriers and guard towers, had reached out into the harbour, separating the pens from the rest of the basin. He racked his brains wondering how they could surmount it.

'Steve! Look out!'

He stopped and glanced back at Patricia, who was pointing into the tunnel ahead. Luigi and the others had halted, watching a powerful torrent of water sweep through the tunnel, sluicing in from the sea outside. It swilled past, ten feet deep, only a few inches from the ledge on which they were standing, and then slowly slacked off and was sucked out again.

'Looks as if something just caved in and let the sea back for a moment,' Lanyon told Patricia. 'These sewers are slightly below water level, but with luck the wind will have lowered the surface enough for us to get out.'

The speed of the air moving past them increased sharply. They rounded a bend and suddenly saw daylight fifty yards ahead, the ragged end of the sewer mouth. Beyond, the sea rose up like a range of massive grey mountains, flecked with huge white caps, driving offshore into the distant blur of spray.

Cautiously they edged towards the sewer's mouth, Luigi waving them on. Ten yards or so of brickwork had collapsed, recessing the mouth below the overhanging ledge of the jetty above. The heavy caissons of the concrete pier rooted down through the now exposed mud flats. Luigi pointed to the right towards the sub-pens, and Lanyon saw that the breakwater had been smashed and lay on its side in huge battered sections a hundred yards out in the harbour.

'We leave you here,' the interpreter told him. 'To the right, one hundred metres, you get into the dock. Then O.K.'

Lanyon nodded, took Patricia's arm. Leaning over the edge of the sewer, where the last of the seawater was dripping out, he lowered her down to the mud flat ten feet below, letting her drop when she was a few feet off the ground. She sank to her knees in the slimy ooze, paddled slowly through the mud towards the firmer ground under the sewer, supporting herself against the concrete pillars.

Lanyon turned to Luigi, held his square hand firmly and patted his shoulder.

The big man smiled back then pulled the .45 out of his belt and passed it to Lanyon.

Lanyon turned to the interpreter. 'Tell him I'll vote for him if he'll run as next mayor of Genoa.'

Luigi roared, slapped Lanyon on the shoulder and helped him down over the edge of the sewer.

Lanyon dropped up to his thighs in the soft black mud, waved to the figures above for the last time and waded slowly between the pillars to where Patricia was sheltering on a narrow flat against the rear wall of the pier. He took her arm and they edged along the wall, straddling the tangle of twisted girders that were all that remained of the breakwater. Inside the submarine base they were still sheltered by the overhang of the pier, but the air roaring past sucked at them like a giant vacuum.

They clung to the tangled seaweed fronds and barnacles encrusted to the pillars, and Lanyon pointed out the jutting roof of the first sub-pen fifty yards away. With a jolt of fear he realized that the receding sea had exposed the floor of the pen, and that although this would enable them to get into the pens it meant that there might be insufficient water to float out the *Terrapin*. Fortunately the sub was berthed in the farthest of the semicircle of pens, and the wind would be driving the sea across it.

They reached the first pen and pulled themselves around the lip into the gateway, their feet gripping the concrete floor. Ahead of them the steel shutters towered up to the roof. They ran over to the grille, and through the slits Lanyon could see the stranded hull of one of the K-class subs, lying on its side in the dim grey light.

The vanes of the grille were open, leaving two-foot gaps. Lanyon lifted Patricia up onto the lowest gap, and she clambered through into the great hull of the pen. Lanyon followed her and they ran under the towering underbelly of the stranded submarine, its moorings snapped and hanging loose, conning tower tilted at a forty-five degree angle.

They reached the stairway to the cargo pier, climbed up

110

past the submarine, and then turned into the corridor that led to the control deck at the far end of the pen.

'Well, Pat, we've got this far,' Lanyon said, as they paused in the corridor to regain their breath. He pulled the torch from his jacket, switched it on.

'Doesn't look as if there's anyone around, Steve. Do you think the *Terrapin* will still be here?'

'God knows. If not, we'll come back and sit the storm out in the big K-boat.'

They reached the control deck, peered into the abandoned offices. The heavy concrete walls of the base were still holding without any difficulty, but somewhere a ventilator had collapsed and air poured through the vents, blowing the papers off the desks and shelves. Litter lay everywhere, drawers pulled out, water dispensers smashed, broken suitcases strewn about the floor.

'Left in a hurry,' Lanyon commented. 'Seems to me that this is a pretty good place to sit tight. Where the hell have they all gone?'

They hurried along the dark communications corridor, crossing the control decks of the next three pens. As they passed the fifth the floor suddenly shifted slightly, and Lanyon tripped and collided with the wall.

'Good God, don't tell me it can move even this place! The sea must be breaking over the entrance to the pen, driving the whole unit back into the shore.'

'Come on, Steve, let's hurry,' Patricia said. She held onto his arm as they ran down the corridor. They stumbled into the last control deck, dived down the stairway into the cargo depot. As they reached the bottom the door out into the jetty opened, lights flooded on and two sailors peered round. They gaped at Lanyon and Patricia, clothes ripped to shreds, covered with thick mud up to their waists, Lanyon's bruised face barely recognizable under his beard. Their hands moved to the revolvers in their holsters, and then one of them jumped to attention and snapped out a salute.

He swung his head through the doorway, shouted out:

'Attention there! Commander Lanyon to come aboard!'

Lanyon put a hand out and squeezed the man's shoulder gratefully, then stepped through onto the narrow pier.

Deep water boiled and swirled into the sub-pen through the open gates, surging down to the far wall 200 yards away.

Riding high on it, deckwork trim, periscopes aligned, was the *Terrapin*!

Paul Matheson waited while Lanyon towelled himself down after the shower and climbed into a clean uniform.

'We're all set to move off, Steve. We've had a last check around the base; there's no one here.'

Lanyon nodded. 'Fine, Paul. By the way, how's the girl who came aboard with me?'

'Miss Olsen? She's O.K., a little shocked but she'll come to. Looks as if you had quite a job getting back here. She's sharing a cabin with the three WAC nurses. Tight squeeze. We've got about sixty extra passengers.'

'Sorry to bring another, Paul. Still, she can have Van Damm's vacancy. If it's any consolation, she's with NBC; she's probably taking all this down in cinemascope. Remember, it's not enough to make history – you've got to arrange for someone to record it for you.'

Lanyon buttoned his shirt up, glancing at the movement signal from Tunis lying on the table.

'Portsmouth, England, eh? Do you think they've got any more corpses for us to collect?'

Matheson shook his head. 'No, I gather they're top air force and embassy VIP's. May even be the ambassador and his family. Where we'll put them I don't know.'

He laughed easily, and Lanyon noticed that Matheson seemed to have filled out considerably over the past few days. There was an air of authority and confidence about him that suggested he had been through his own private ordeal.

Lanyon fingered the movement order. 'Paul, this came through three days ago. Strictly speaking, you should have got under way immediately.'

Matheson shrugged. 'Well, I couldn't leave the skipper behind, could I, Steve?' He hesitated. 'As a matter of fact, two more orders came through when we didn't clear back, followed up by a couple of troubleshooters from the Provost Marshal's unit here. Slight problem there. They could see we were all ready to blow, so I had to, er, use a little bit of old-fashioned persuasion.'

He grinned at Lanyon, and tapped the butt of the .45 stuck in his belt.

Lanyon nodded. 'I wondered what that was for. Thought perhaps you were trying to impress the WACs. Pretty good, Paul. Well, let's go topside and get this rig under way.'

They climbed up into the conning tower, crouched down under the awning stretched across to keep out the spray thrown up off the sides of the pen. At the far end Lanyon could see heavy seas smashing against the open doors, hear the deafening unrelenting roar of the wind screaming past like a dozen express trains.

The entire pen was shifting sideways under the impact of the seas breaking across it, and large crack spilt the roof and walls. The *Terrapin* was moored well back in the pen, double lines of truck tyres lashed to her hull to protect her from the pier.

The last lines were cast off, and they began to edge ahead under the big diesels, churning a boiling wake of foam and black water behind the twin screws.

They swung out into the centre of the pen, fifty yards from the entrance, bows breaking out of the water as swells rode in from the sea, lifting the sub almost to the roof.

Lanyon was checking the forward elevator trim when

Matheson suddenly punched him on the shoulder. He looked up quickly as the helmsman shouted and pointed forward to the entrance.

A huge section of the roof, the full width of the pen and forty feet across, was tipping slowly downward crushing the two steel gates like chicken wire. Through the wide crack mountainous seas burst like floodwater through a collapsing dam, splashing across the bows of the *Terrapin*.

'Full astern! Full astern!' Lanyon roared into the mouth tube, hanging onto the edge of the well as the diesels reversed and wrenched the sub back into its wake. They moved fifty yards, and then Lanyon held the *Terrapin* and watched as the collapsing roof section anchored itself in the jaws of the entrance, hanging vertically from the reinforcing roof girders, wedged firmly by the driving seas.

Matheson pounded on the edge of the well, frustration and anger overriding his hysteria. 'We're trapped, Steve, for God's sake! We'll never move it!'

Lanyon ignored him, picked up the mouth tube. 'Starboard torpedo station! Alert! Charge No. 2 tube with main HE heads.'

Waiting for the ready signal, he turned to Matheson. 'We'll blast our way out, Paul. That roof section is at least fifteen feet thick, must weigh about five hundred tons. It's our only chance.'

At the ready signal he backed the *Terrapin* astern right up against the rear wall, so that 150 yards of clear water separated them from the entrance. Then, lining the bows carefully on target, he rapped into the tube, 'Compressors sealed. Discharge vent open.' He paused as the bows swerved slightly, then realigned on the target. 'Fire!'

The torpedo burst from its vent in a rush of bubbles, burrowed rapidly through the water three feet below the surface, moving like an enormous shark. Lanyon watched it until it was twenty yards from the blocked entrance, then crouched down, shouting to the others.

They hit the floor, and he seized the mouth tube and yelled, 'Full ahead! Full ahead!'

As the screws thrashed and bit in, kicking the *Terrapin* forward, the torpedo exploded against its target. There was a vivid white flash that filled the pen, followed by a colossal eruption of exploding concrete and water which burst out of its mouth like a cork from a champagne bottle. Simultaneously a fifteen-foot-high wave swept down the length of the pen, a massive breaker that carried with it a foaming jetsam of concrete and metal. Full ahead, the *Terrapin* was moving at fifteen knots as they met halfway down the pen. It slowed briefly under the impact of the wave, its conning tower glancing off the walls and carrying away a section of the pier. Then it surged forward again, heading smoothly through the gaping mouth of the entrance into the harbour. For a moment its bow rose up steeply under the writhing swells, then sank cleanly into the deep basin, its tower and stern quickly vanishing in a roar of escaping air.

At last the pyramid was complete.

Sliding painfully down its smooth slopes, the few remaining workers dismantled the battered forms, letting their equipment lie where it fell at the foot of the pyramid. One by one, peering up briefly at the grey apex shining above them into the black reeling air, they made their way over to a single trap door sunk into a shaft between the two ramparts. Quickly they disappeared from view, until only a single figure remained, in the shadow of the buckling windshields. For a moment he stood in the shower of dust carried over the shields a hundred feet above, his body swaying in the air exploding around him. Then he too turned and stepped through the trap door, sealing it behind him.

The wind mounted. Raging into the shields, it tore at the plates, snapping the hawsers one by one, cracking the concrete pylons at their bases, driving through the great rents.

Suddenly the pressure became too great. With a gargantuan paroxysm the shattered screen exploded and the splitting plates careened away into the air, bouncing off the sides of the pyramid, dragging with them the frayed remnants of the tangled hawsers, the roots of the pylons and buttresses. No longer protected, the lines of vehicles parked in the lee of the screens dragged and crashed into each other, and finally broke loose, rolling end over end across the lower slopes of the pyramid, rapidly picking up speed, and then spinning away into the darkness with the flying sky.

Now only the pyramid remained.

Chapter 6

Death in a Bunker

Pausing in the doorway to allow the shower of plaster falling from the ceiling to spend itself, Marshall stepped through into the Intelligence Unit. A skeleton staff of three – Andrew Symington, a corporal and one of the navy typists – sat in the dim light of the emergency bunker, surrounded by the jumble of teletypes, radio consoles and TV screens. The scene reminded Marshall of the last hours in Hitler's führer bunker. Discarded bulletins and typed memos lay around everywhere, a clutter of unwashed teacups stood on the lid of a forgotten suitcase, cigarette ash spilled across the desks.

Above the chatter of the teletypes and the muted cross-talk of the R/T he could hear the sounds of the wind echoing through the ventilator shaft that reached up to the Mall sixty feet above. Almost everyone had gone now. The last War Office and COE personnel had left in their Centurions early that morning for the peripheral command posts. Admiralty Arch had collapsed half an hour later, pulling down with it the complex of offices that had housed COE for the previous three weeks. Intelligence was by now a luxury that would soon be dispensed with.

The wind had reached 250 mph and the organized resistance left was more interested in securing the minimal survival necessities – food, warmth and fifty feet of concrete overhead – than in finding out what the rest of the world was doing, knowing full well that everywhere people were doing exactly the same thing. Civilization was hiding. The earth itself was being stripped to its seams, almost literally

– six feet of topsoil were now travelling through the air.

He sat down on the desk behind Symington, patted the plump bald man on his shoulder, then waved at the other two. The girl wore headphones over her straggling hair, and was too harassed answering the calls coming in endlessly from mobile cars and units trapped in basements and deep shelters to have had any time to look after her appearance, attractive as she had once been (Marshall had deliberately kept her on at COE as a morale booster) but when she saw him she ran a hand over her hair and gave him a brave smile.

'How's it going, Andrew?'

Symington sat back, massaged his eyes for a moment before replying. He looked exhausted and ashen faced, but managed a thin smile.

'Well, chief, I guess we can start getting ready to surrender. Looks to me as if the war's over.'

Marshall laughed. 'I was just thinking the place feels as if the Russians are two hundred yards away. How are the PM and the Chief of Staff?'

'They reached Leytonheath a couple of hours ago. The mine at Sutton Coldfield had been flooded by underground springs – water must have driven through a fault leading in from the North Sea – so they've been forced to dig into the shelters at the airfield. They're O.K. there for three weeks, but after that there'll have to be a general election.'

A wry smile crossed Marshall's face. For a moment he looked reflectively at Symington, then said: 'What's the latest from the Met. people? Any hope of a breakthrough on the weather front?'

Symington shrugged. 'They went off the air about an hour ago. Pulled out to Dulwich. I don't think they've known any more for the last week than you or I. Just about all they've done is lick their fingers and hold them over their heads. The latest wind speed is 255. That's an increase of 4.7 over 11 a.m. yesterday.'

'An effective drop, though,' Marshall said hopefully.

'Yes, but it's accounted for by the tremendous mass of soil particles being carried. The sky's jet black now.'

'What about overseas?'

'Had a signal in from a USAF field in New Jersey. Apparently New York is a total write-off. Manhattan's under hundred-foot waves, most of the big skyscrapers and office blocks are down. Empire State Building toppled like a falling chimney stack. Same story everywhere else. Casualty lists in the millions. Paris, Berlin, Rome – nothing but rubble, people hanging on in cellars.'

The bunker shuddered under the impact of a building falling above, like a depth charge shaking a submarine. The bulbs danced on the ends of their flexes. Dust filtered down from the ceiling. Involuntarily Marshall's eyes moved to the mouth of the ventilator shaft, his mind crossing the interval of compacted clay up to the garage in the basement above where the big super-tractor waited to take him to safety.

The corporal by the TV screens spoke up. 'When do we pack this lot in, sir?' he asked anxiously. 'Seems to me we're cutting it a bit fine.'

'Don't worry,' Marshall told him. 'We'll get out safely enough. Let's try to hang on here as long as we can. You three are just about the only intact intelligence outfit still operating in the whole of Europe.' There was a hint of pride in Marshall's voice, the pride of a man who has created a perfect team and hates to see it disbanded even after it's outlived its purpose. He gave them all a wide encouraging grin. 'You never know, Crighton; you may be the first person to see the wind reach its peak and slack off.'

Symington shifted a stack of teletype memos, spread them out on his desk, anchoring them from the draught with a stack of pennies.

'This is the provincial set-up. Birmingham: an estimated 300,000 people are sheltering in the coal mines around the city. Ninety-nine per cent of the city is down.

119

Tremendous fires from the refineries at West Bromwich swept across the ruins yesterday, finished off what little the wind had left. Estimated casualties: 200,000.'

'Sounds low,' Marshall commented dourly.

'Probably is. Homo sapiens is pretty tenacious, but if London is any guide most people went down into their basements with one packet of sandwiches and a thermos of cocoa.' He went on, 'Manchester: heavy casualties were caused yesterday when the roof of London Road station caved in. For some reason the authorities have been concentrating people there, there were something like 20,000 packed between the platforms.'

Marshall nodded while Symington continued in a low steady voice. There seemed to be a depressing uniformity about the reports. When he had heard one he had heard them all. The same picture emerged; the entire population of one of the world's most highly industrialized nations, equipped with an elaborate communications and transport system, huge stores of fuel and food, large armed services, yet caught completely unprepared by a comparatively slight increase in one of the oldest constants of its natural environment.

On the whole, people had shown less resourcefulness and flexibility, less foresight, than a wild bird or animal would. Their basic survival instincts had been so dulled, so overlaid by mechanisms designed to serve secondary appetites, that they were totally unable to protect themselves. As Symington had implied, they were the helpless victims of a deep-rooted optimism about their right to survival, their dominance of the natural order which would guarantee them against everything but their own folly, so that they had made gross assumptions about their own superiority.

Now they were paying the price for this, in truth reaping the whirlwind!

He listened to Symington complete the picture.

'A few navy units are operating bases around the Portsmouth and Plymouth areas – the defences and arsenals there are tunnelled deep underground, but in general military control is breaking down. Rescue operations are virtually over. There are a few army patrols with the crowds in the London Underground system, but how long they can keep command is anybody's guess.'

Marshall nodded. He moved across to the bank of TV receivers. There were six of them, relaying pictures transmitted from automatic cameras mounted in sealed concrete towers that Marshall had had built at points all over London. The sets were labelled: Campden Hill, Westminster, Hampstead, Mile End Road, Battersea, Waterloo. The pictures flickered and were lashed with interference patterns, but the scenes they revealed were plain enough. The right-hand screen, labelled Mile End Road, was blank, and the corporal was adjusting the controls in an effort to get a picture.

Marshall studied one of the other screens, then tapped Crighton on the shoulder.

'I shouldn't bother.' He indicated the Hampstead screen, pointed through the blur of dust swept off the shattered rooftops. The camera was traversing automatically from left to right in three-second sweeps; as it neared its leftward stop Marshall put his finger on the screen, pointing to a stub of grey concrete sticking up above the desolation several miles away on the horizon. As the dust-storm cleared for a moment, revealing the rectangular outlines of the Mile End tower, they could see that a pile of debris lay across its waist, the remains of a ten-storey building that had been carried bodily across the ground. The tower was still standing, but the camera turret, fifty feet above ground, had been snapped off.

Marshall switched off the set, then sat down in front of the screen covering the Westminster area. Its transmitting tower was mounted on a traffic island at the bottom of

Whitehall only a few hundred yards from where they were sitting. It had been fitted with a 180 degree traverse, and was pointing up Whitehall towards Trafalgar Square. The road had disappeared below enormous mounds of rubble driven across the pavement from the shells of the ministries on the eastern side. The War Office and Ministry of Agriculture were down. Beyond them, the spires of Whitehall Court had vanished; only spurs of masonry were sticking up against the backdrop of the blackened sky.

The camera swung, following the battered remains of a double-decker bus rolling across the rubble. Tossed over the ruins of the Foreign Office and Downing Street, it bounced off the remains of the Home Office portico and then was carried away across St James's Park. Along the horizon were the low ragged outlines of the National Gallery and the clubs down Pall Mall, with here and there the gaunt rectangular outline of a hotel or office block.

Marshall watched the last moments of the Piccadilly Hotel. The intervening area, Haymarket and the south side of the Circus, was down, and the hotel was standing out alone above the tempest. The colonnade between the wings was still intact, but just as the camera moved across it two of the columns buckled and crashed back into the face of the hotel, driving tremendous rents through the wall. Instantly, before the camera had time to move away, the entire front of the hotel collapsed in an explosion of dust and masonry. One of the wings tipped over and then crashed to the ground, carrying with it the remains of a small office block that had sheltered behind it. The other wing rode high above the chaos like the bows of a greater liner breasting a vast sea, and then slipped and cascaded to the ground in a soundless avalanche.

As the camera swung full left onto the Houses of Parliament, Marshall saw heavy waves breaking among the ruins of the Lords. Driven into the estuary by the wind, powerful seas were flooding into the Thames and being carried up as far as Windsor, sweeping away the locks and spilling over the banks, where they completed the task of destruction started by the wind. The time-familiar river façade of Westminster had vanished, and high seas washed across the ragged lines of foundation stones, spilling over the supine remains of Big Ben, stripping the clock faces as they lay among the rubble in Palace Yard.

Suddenly the corporal jumped forward, pointing to the set receiving the Hammersmith picture.

'Sir! Quickly! They're trying to come out!'

They crowded around the set, watching the screen. The camera was mounted over Hammersmith Broadway. Directly below in the street, a hundred feet away from them, was the entrance to Hammersmith Underground. The tall office buildings in the street were down to their first storeys, walls poking up through piles of rubble, but the entrance to the station had been fortified with a heavy concrete breastwork that jutted out into the roadway, three circular doors fitted into its domed roof.

These were open now, and emerging from them was a press of struggling people, fighting and pulling past each other in a frantic effort to escape from the station. The doorways were packed with them, some peering out hesitantly when they reached the entrance, then being propelled out into the open street by the pressure of the mob behind them.

Like petals torn from a wind-blown flower they detached themselves from the doorways, took a few helpless steps out into the street and were whipped off their feet and hurled across the road, bouncing head over heels like sacks of feathers that burst and disintegrated as they ripped into the ragged teeth of reinforcing bars protruding from the debris.

The camera swung away from the scene and pointed eastward into the face of the storm, the panorama obscured by the clouds of flying stones that poured into the face of the camera like countless machine-gun tracers in a heavy bombardment.

Symington was sitting limply in his chair, grimly watching the screen. On the other side of the table Crighton and the Wren typist watched silently, their faces grey and pinched. Above them the light bulbs shook spasmodically as the bunker trembled, illuminating the thin dust falling from the ceiling. It drifted slowly across the room to the mouth of the ventilator shaft, where it swirled away.

The camera returned to the Underground station. The stream of people were still trying to get out, but somehow they had realized the futility of stepping straight into the wind and were trying to make their way along the protecting wall of the concrete breastwork. But no sooner had they gone ten or fifteen feet when they again felt the full undiminished force of the wind stream and were twisted helplessly from their hand holds and spun away into the air.

Marshall slammed one fist into the other. 'What are they trying to do?' he shouted in exasperation. 'Why don't the fools stay where they are, for God's sake?'

Symington shook his head slowly. 'The tunnels must be flooded. The river's only half a mile away and water's probably pumping in under enormous pressure.' He glanced up at Marshall, smiled bleakly. 'Or maybe they're just worn out, terrified to the point where escape is the only possible solution, even if it's just escape to death.'

Marshall nodded, then glanced at his watch. He looked around the room for a moment, taking in each of his three companions, nodded to them and began to move for the door where banks of teletypes stood against the wall.

'Not much coming through,' he said to Symington. 'Looks as if we ought to start pulling out. Might take anything up to a couple of days to reach the US base at Brandon Hall. No point in trying to be heroes. Get in touch with them and see if traffic there can pick us up today. I'll look in again in half an hour.'

He made his way quickly along the darkened corridor to the small stairway at the end of the floor, then hurried up it

124

to the level above. His office was half-way down, backing onto the elevator shaft and emergency exit.

Unlocking the door, he let himself in. Deborah Mason, a heavy trench coat belted around her trim waist, was sitting on the sofa next to her suitcase. She stood up as he came in, put her arms on Marshall's shoulders.

'Are you ready now, Simon?' she asked anxiously. 'I can't wait to get out of here.'

Marshall held her close to him and smiled into her smooth face, touching her lips lightly with his own. 'Don't worry, darling. All set now.'

The small room was stacked with gear. A carton of gas masks and an R/T set cluttered the desk, crates and suitcases stood against the walls. First testing the door to make certain it was locked, Marshall sat down at his desk and dialled the transport shelter above.

'Kroll?' he asked in a low voice. 'Marshall here. Get ready to pull out in about ten minutes.' He paused, looking away from Deborah and dropping his voice. 'Meanwhile, can you come down to my office? Take the rear stairway by the elevator shaft. I'll need your help with something.'

Slipping the phone back into its cradle, Marshall glanced up at Deborah, who was watching him suspiciously, her mouth fretting slightly.

'Simon, why do you want Kroll to come down here?'

Marshall began to shrug, but Deborah cut in: 'Symington and the other two are coming with us, aren't they? You're not going to leave him behind?'

'Symington? Of course not, darling. He's invaluable to us. But we'll need Kroll to help persuade him to come along.'

He stood up and walked over to one of the suitcases, but Deborah stopped him.

'What about Crighton and the girl?' she pressed. 'You're not going to leave them, or try anything –'

Marshall hesitated, looking Deborah in the face, his eyes motionless.

'Simon!' Deborah seized his arms. 'They've worked for you for months; both of them trust you completely. You can't just throw their lives away. Hardoon can use them somewhere.'

Marshall clenched his teeth, pushed Deborah away. 'For heaven's sake, Deborah, don't start sentimentalizing. I hate to do it, but these are tough times. People are dying out there by the million. Are you willing to swap places with one of them?'

'No, I'm not,' Deborah said firmly, 'but that's not the point, is it? You've got a place for them.'

'In the Titan, yes. But at the Tower – I can't be sure. Hardoon is unpredictable; I've no real authority with him. I'd leave them here, but they'll put out an alert within five minutes and we'd be picked up before we'd gone ten miles.' He looked down at Deborah, her mouth clenched determinedly, then burst out in a growl of irritation:

'All right then, I'll take a chance. It's a hell of a risk, though.'

He picked up the suitcase, carried it over to the sofa. The case was of medium size, with heavy metal ribs that appeared to have been mounted at a date later than its original manufacture.

Taking a keychain from his pocket, Marshall opened the two locks and carefully raised the lid. Inside was a small vhf radio transceiver, equipped with a powerful scrambler.

Marshall switched on the scrambler, then reached down to the floor behind the sofa and picked up a long piece of loose wire. The end had been fitted with a plug and he clipped this into the aerial socket of the transceiver. Following the wire behind the sofa to the corner, he traced it along the skirting board behind his desk to the emergency door, where it disappeared through a small aperture.

126

Satisfied, he returned to the set, unwound a power lead and plugged it into his desk light. As he switched on he listened to the set hum into life, then quietly adjusted the tuning dial until the red fixed-beam answering bulb lit up. Then he pulled on the headphones and picked up the miniature microphone.

'Hardoon Tower, this is Black Admiral calling Hardoon Tower,' he began to repeat rapidly. Deborah came and stood at his shoulder, and he put his free arm around her.

As the answering call came through, the narrow door behind Marshall's desk opened slowly. A tall, heavily built man in black plastic storm suit and fibreglass helmet stepped softly into the room. His face was hidden by the deep visor of the helmet and the broad metal chin-strap, but between them were a tight scarred mouth, a sharp nose and cheekbones, hard eyes. The man's hands were gloveless, rubber seals at the sleeves of the suit clasping his thick wrists. In the centre of his helmet was a single large white triangle, like a pyramid in profile.

Marshall waved him into the room, gesturing him to lock the door behind him, then crouched over the set.

'. . . tell R.H. we're leaving in about five minutes, estimated time of arrival at the Tower –' he glanced at his watch '– 0400 hours. Everything here is closing down, all government agencies pulled out yesterday. The Titan will carry US Navy insignia – it's too dangerous to move around now without any markings and the only other big tractors are American, so no one will try to stop us. What's that?'

Marshall paused, watching the tall figure of Kroll standing beside him as the question was repeated. 'I'll be bringing them along. They're top communications people; they'll be useful to us. What? There are only three of them. Don't worry, I'll see R.H. personally about it.' Marshall's face began to knot, his deep jaw lengthening as he listened impatiently to the voice in his earphones. He started to say:

'Listen, I don't care what orders R.H. made –' then abruptly uncupped his headphones and switched the set off.

'Bloody fool!' he snapped. 'Who does that operator think he is?' His face clouded with anger, then slowly relaxed. He pulled out the aerial, then folded away the earphones and hand microphone and closed the case.

'Have to watch R.H.' he said reflectively to Kroll. 'He's a tough nut, all right. Just because Communications are taking second place to Construction now the boys at the Tower are starting to get cocky.'

Kroll nodded, almost imperceptibly, as if well used to a maximum conversational economy. 'There's been a lot of reorganization,' he said tersely. 'Big changes, cutting down. Construction's taking a back seat now. Security is head department.'

Marshall said nothing, pensively considering this. 'Who's in charge?' he asked.

Kroll shook his head. His hard face flickered bonily; something reminiscent of a chuckle rasped out. 'R.H., the boss himself.' He was eyeing Deborah up and down with interest, and she backed away from him slightly. Kroll broke off and glanced around the office. 'Let's get a move on, eh?' he added curtly.

Marshall carried the suitcase over to the desk, noting the change in Kroll's manner. 'Good idea,' he agreed. 'Thanks for all the news. By the way, what department are you in now? Security? I take it you've been promoted.'

Kroll nodded, watching Marshall without a hint of deference. He moved towards the outer door, jerked a thumb in the direction of the corridor. 'Where do the others hang out? Down on the bottom level?'

'Hold on.' Marshall turned to Deborah, took her by the arm and steered her towards the emergency door. 'Darling, there's bound to be a little rough stuff here. You go ahead upstairs. Everything will have quieted down by the time we reach you.'

The girl hesitated, but Marshall smiled at her. 'Believe me, Deborah, I give you my word they'll come with us. See you in a moment.'

As she stepped through the doorway, apparently satisfied by his assurance, Marshall turned back to Kroll.

'You stay here. I'll bring them up.'

Kroll held his hand on the doorknob, looking over his shoulder at Marshall. The two big men seemed to fill the tiny office.

Kroll raised one shoulder slightly, listening to the sounds of Deborah's feet disappear up the stairway. 'Why bother?' he asked laconically. 'Fix them down there. Don't want to leave a lot of mess around your office. Somebody might stumble in and find them.'

Marshall reached past Kroll, pressed his elbow firmly against Kroll's arm and edged his hand off the knob.

'I'm taking them with me,' he said quietly. 'We're not fixing them up here or anywhere else.' He opened the door to find it lodged almost immediately against Kroll's black leather boot. Marshall looked down at the steel toecap, placed squarely in his path, then straightened his shoulders and peered hard at Kroll, dull anger pounding in his temples.

'Get away from that door!' he snapped. 'What the hell do you think you're playing at?'

He started to lean his shoulder against Kroll's, but Kroll suddenly swung around with his back to the door and slammed it shut with a sharp kick of the other heel.

He eyed Marshall carefully. 'Hold it, Marshall. You got your orders from the Tower two minutes ago. R.H. isn't fooling around.'

Marshall shook his head. 'Listen, Kroll, just shut up and take your orders from me. I'll deal with R.H. when I reach the Tower. Meanwhile I don't want you telling me what to do. I'm taking these three people back with us.'

'What for? You'll never get them in. R.H. just sealed

129

out two hundred workers in Construction who've been on the Tower right from the beginning.'

Marshall ignored him, was about to seize Kroll's shoulder and wrench him away from the door when there was a tap on the far side of the frosted glass. Kroll dived back, his right hand sliding swiftly in the centre vent of his jacket and emerging a fraction of a second later with a heavy .45 automatic, a toy in his enormous fist.

Marshall waved him into the corner behind the door, then opened it to find Symington standing there, blinking in the bright light, dust streaks on his bald domed head.

'Hello, Andrew. What's the problem?' Marshall backed sideways into the office, drawing Symington after him. Kroll was behind the door.

'Sorry to bother you, chief,' Symington began to explain. 'Crighton heard someone come down the emergency exit and went up to the transport bay. Apparently there's one of those big American –' He broke off noticing the huge figure of Kroll poised behind him. 'What's going –' he began to say, then tried helplessly to back into the corridor as Kroll grabbed him by the shoulder with his left hand and wrenched him back off his feet, his right hand swinging the heavy barrel of the automatic at his head.

The blow had the full lethal power of Kroll's powerful physique behind it. Marshall dived for the gun hand, at the same time seizing Symington by the back of the neck and forcing him to the floor. He and Kroll locked arms and grappled with each other, as Symington struggled at their feet between them. Suddenly they sprang apart. Symington darted quickly through the doorway before the two big men could collect themselves, and slammed it in front of them.

Before Marshall could stop him, Kroll had fired through the frosted glass at the blurring image moving down the corridor. The sound of the shot roared out like an exploding bomb in the confined office. Shattered glass spat against the walls of the corridor. Through the aperture Marshall saw

Symington kicked headlong by the force of the bullet, then slammed crookedly onto his face as if flung from a speeding car.

Kroll pulled back the door and dived out into the corridor. With Marshall following him, he raced across to where Symington was lying, glanced cursorily at the figure at his feet, then started to move down the corridor, the automatic raised steadily in front of him.

Marshall knelt down beside Symington. In the dim light he felt the warm wet patch spreading from the wound just below his left shoulder blade. He turned Symington over, saw that he was breathing in short exhausted pants. Fortunately the bullet had struck him obliquely, channelling out a three-inch-long furrow without penetrating the rib cage. Marshall sat Symington up, dragged him back into the office and propped him against the sofa.

Behind him the emergency door opened and Deborah peered around, her eyes wide with alarm.

'Simon, what's happening?' She gaped down at Symington uncomprehendingly. 'You promised –'

Marshall pulled her down to the sofa.

'Stay with him, see what you can do. I think he's all right. Kroll's going crazy. I've got to stop him before he kills the other two.'

As he re-entered the corridor Kroll was stepping cautiously down the stairway. Marshall pulled the short-barrelled .38 from his shoulder holster. Thumbing off the safety catch, he moved forward after Kroll.

Kroll's helmeted head had just disappeared down the short stairway when a second shot roared out from the floor below. Crighton and the Wren typist were both armed, like Marshall, with COE .38's issued to protect them from hunger-maddened intruders.

He heard Kroll's .45 fire once, followed by two sharper reports from the communications room at the far end. He slid carefully down the steps, searching for Kroll's form among the shadows and angles of the corridor, then heard the soft pad of his rubber soles moving towards the service corridor which ringed the offices and provided a rear entrance to the emergency elevator.

Through the open doorway of the communications room Marshall caught a glimpse of Crighton's brown uniform crouched behind the line of teletypes. He ducked back as the .38 flashed out.

The service corridor led off immediately at his left, turning at right angles around the offices. Marshall edged the revolver forward, barrel pointed at the ceiling. He fired twice in quick succession, then dived across the exposed interval into the shelter of the service corridor.

As he caught his breath he heard Crighton fire again at the staircase and then shout something at the girl, his words lost in the roaring echoes.

Following Kroll, Marshall moved quickly down the darkened service corridor, peering briefly into the first of the offices, a clutter of desks under the dim glow of the single storm bulb over the doorway.

A second empty office and the elevator shaft separated him from the communications room at the far end. He edged carefully around the blind corners of the shaft. Fortunately the emergency doorway into the service corridor was blocked by the TV transmitters. As soon as they saw Kroll open it Crighton and the girl would empty their guns through the thin plywood.

Marshall turned the final angle around the shaft and to his surprise found it empty. The emergency door was slightly open; a narrow strip of light crossed the corridor.

Stepping over to it, Marshall peered through.

The room was empty. Dull reflections of the TV screens swung slowly to and fro across the ceiling, but Crighton and the girl had gone.

Suddenly, from the main corridor, two shots roared out heavily, followed by a sharp cry of terror, and then, an agonizing second later, by a third shot. The sounds stunned the air. Flashes of light reflected off the glass panels of the open doorway.

Wrenching open the emergency door, Marshall kicked back a table carrying two of the TV sets, ran quickly across the room.

Crighton and the girl lay together in the corridor, Crighton face downward with his head tilted against the wall, hands raised in front of him. The girl was crumpled untidily behind him, unkempt hair over her face, her skirt around her waist.

Beyond them, waiting for Marshall by the staircase, stood the black figure of Kroll, the automatic jutting from his hand.

'Thanks for covering me,' he said thickly. He pointed to the office near the stairway. 'I was in there. Thought they'd try to make a dash for it when they heard you go around the side.'

The drab air of the bunker was stained with sharp sweet fumes that stung Marshall's eyes. He bent down over the bodies, checked them carefully. A damp strip of handkerchief was clenched in the girl's hand like a dead flower. For a long moment he stared at it, then gradually became aware of Kroll's boots two or three feet away from him.

He started to get up, then saw the automatic in Kroll's hand, levelled at his face. The heavy barrel followed him unwaveringly. Kroll's head was low between his shoulders, his eyes hidden behind the visor of his helmet.

Marshall felt his courage ebbing. 'What's happening, Kroll?' he managed to say in a steady voice. He moved towards Kroll, who stepped back and let him pass, training the .45 on Marshall's head.

'Sorry, Marshall,' he said flatly. 'R.H.'

'What? Hardoon?' Marshall hesitated, estimating the distance to the stairway. Kroll was a few paces behind him. So Hardoon had decided to dispense with him, now that

Marshall had served his purpose! He should have realized this when Kroll had been sent to collect them. 'Don't be crazy,' he said. 'You must have your wires crossed.'

When he was six feet from the stairway he suddenly dived forward, swerving from side to side, and managed to put his left hand on the stair rail.

Aiming carefully, Kroll shot him twice, first in the back, the impact of the bullet lifting Marshall onto the bottom step and knocking him off his feet, the second shot into his stomach as he toppled around, his great body uncontrollable, his arms swinging like windmills. He stumbled past Kroll, spun heavily against the wall and crashed downward into a corner.

He was about ten feet from Kroll, who waited quietly until the narrow stream of blood meandering across the concrete floor finally reached his feet, then made his way quickly up the staircase.

'Simon!'

The girl was crouched behind the door, fingers over her face. As she saw Kroll she screamed and backed away from him, almost tripping over the recumbent figure of Andrew Symington, half conscious on the floor by the sofa.

Kroll jerked the .45 back into his jacket, then stepped over to Deborah, cornering her behind the desk.

'Where is he?' she shouted at him. 'Simon? What have you –'

Kroll knocked her against the wall with the back of his hand, forced her to the floor.

'Shut up!' he snarled. 'Crazy yapping!'

He listened carefully to the sounds shifting around the bunker, kicking the girl sharply with his boot when her blubbering interrupted him, then picked up the phone.

As he waited he looked down at Deborah, and his right hand edged back towards the .45. His fingers flexed around the heavy butt, drawing it out.

He searched for the back of Deborah's neck, then noticed the auburn curls tipping forward over her head. They were soft and wispy, more delicate than anything Kroll had ever seen. Like a huge bull entranced by a butterfly, he watched them, fascinated, feeling his blood thicken, ignoring the voice on the phone.

His hand relaxed and withdrew from his jacket.

'All set,' he said slowly into the phone. 'Just one of them.' He glanced down at Deborah. 'I'll be about ten minutes.'

Lurching painfully, Marshall dragged himself into the darkened communications room, heaved up onto his feet and then slumped into a chair in front of the radio transmitter. For a few minutes he coughed uncontrollably, fighting for air, his body drowning in the enormous lake of ice which filled his chest. As he rolled helplessly from side to side his eyes stared at the blood eddying across the floor below the chair. The trail led back into the corridor, past the two bodies to the stairway. How many hours had elapsed since he had first set out for the transmitter he could no longer remember, but the sight of the bodies revived him momentarily, making him realize that his great strength was ebbing rapidly, and he leaned forward on his elbows and began to switch on the set.

Around him the bunker was silent. The ventilator system had been turned off and the air was stale and motionless, still stained by the acrid fumes of the cordite. Along the wall behind him the teletypes were at last quiet, the sole sounds provided by the low hum of the TV sets. Only two of the screens showed a picture, their reflections swinging left and right across the dark ceiling.

Fumbling helplessly, Marshall paused to steady himself, trying to conserve what little air he could force into his lungs. The wound through his chest wall felt as wide as a lance blade, each breath turning it between his shattered ribs.

Half an hour later, when he had almost gone, the set came alive between his fingers. Seizing the microphone with both hands, he rammed it to his lips, began to speak into it carefully, doggedly repeating his message over and over again, heedless of the replies interrupting him from the other end, until its meaning had gone and it became an insane gabble.

When he had finally finished, his voice a whisper, he let the microphone fall through his fingers to the floor, then jerked his chair slightly and faced the TV screens. Only one picture was being transmitted now, a white blur of flickering dust that crossed the screen from left to right, unvarying in its speed and direction.

The focus of his eyes fading, Marshall lay back, watching it blindly. His grey handsome face was almost in repose, the skin hollowing around his eyes and temples, draining his lips. Unaware of his own breathing, he felt himself sink down towards the bottom of the ice lake. Around him the stale air grew steadily colder. A few sounds shifted somewhere above in the empty bunker, echoing down the silent ventilator shafts and through the deserted corridors of his end.

Chapter 7

The Gateways of the Whirlwind

'How is he?'

'Not too bad. Mild concussion, hairline fracture above the right ear. Second-degree burns to the palms and soles.'

'He'll pull through, though?'

'Oh, yes. If we do, he will.'

The voices drifted away. Donald Maitland stirred pleasantly, half asleep, almost enjoying the sensation of drowsy warmth coupled with a slight nausea. Now and then the voices would return. Sometimes he could only hear the rise and fall of their tones as they moved among the patients; at other times, when they discussed his own case, standing over him, he could hear them plainly.

He was on the mend, at least. Turning lazily, he tried to make himself comfortable, tried to feel the stiff caress of crisp sheets against his face.

Yet he could never find them. Whenever he searched, the bed and pillow were hard and unyielding as he realized his hands were in plaster casts.

He wished he could wake. Then sleep would come again, numbing the pain in his head and across his shoulders, dulling the nausea that made him want to vomit.

'Looks a lot better. Don't you agree?'

'No doubt about it. But those burns are a little worrying. How the hell did he get them?'

'Forget exactly. I think he was trapped in the boiler room at the generating station. They may be carbide burns . . .'

Their voices moved away as consciousness returned, paused and then faded. Maitland stretched and flexed his

legs, pressed his feet against the foot of the bed.
Burns?

How? He remembered being trapped in the Underground station at Knightsbridge. Had he been transferred to another hospital centre, perhaps had his identity confused?

The voices drifted behind him, murmuring over another patient. Maitland felt cold, his head pounded. He wanted to call them, tell them they were over-confident.

They moved off slowly, their voices lost in the sounds of some enormous fan.

Burns?

With an effort, he opened his eyes, slowly moved his head. He was blind!

He sat up and groped at the bed around him, half expecting them to come back, to feel restraining hands press him back onto the pillow, hear the first words of consolation.

He picked up something large and angular, heavy in his hand.

A brick!

He nestled it between his knees. What was this doing in bed with him? His fingers groped at its rough surface, pulling away pieces of fine mortar.

He looked around, hoping to attract their attention, but their voices had vanished: the ward was silent.

Exhausted suddenly, he dropped the brick, lay back limply.

Instantly the voices returned.

'How did the grafts come along?'

'Very well, all in all. We'll take his arms out of the cradle tomorrow. . . .'

Maitland smiled to himself. Perhaps they were in darkness, unable to see that his hands were under the sheet.

He flexed his fingers, picked another object off the bed. A torch.

Instinctively, he switched it on.

The beam filled his tiny cubicle, illuminating piles of

shattered bricks on either side of him, a concrete beam two feet broad running across his knees, supporting a large sign.

Huge letters ran along it. They read: CLEARANCE SALE.

For a moment Maitland stared at it, sitting upright, tracing the letters with his fingers.

Then, abruptly assembling his mind again, he shone the torch around himself.

So he was not in a hospital as he had imagined, but still trapped in the tunnel. The voices, the diagnoses, the warm bed, had all been products of fantasy, wish fulfilments summoned by his exhausted body.

His head throbbed. Maitland shone the torch at his hands, kneading the broken skin. He was half surprised to see that they were not badly burned, and wondered why his mind should have produced this curious piece of circumstantial detail. Perhaps he had remembered a case history of one of his former patients.

Looking around him, he searched for some possible exit, but the narrow space in which he lay seemed completely sealed.

Exhausted, he lay back, still shining the torch.

'I think we can move him out tomorrow. How do you feel?'

'Pretty good, thank you, sir. I'm very grateful to you. Any news about the wind?'

The voices had returned. Even the patient had now joined in. Too tired to understand why these delusions should persist so powerfully even when he was fully conscious, Maitland lay back, rotating his head to find a more comfortable position.

He listened interestedly to the voices, the first hallucinatory agents he had ever encountered, his mind automatically analysing them.

Moving his head, he noticed that a wide circular shaft about two feet in diameter formed part of his pillow. It moved diagonally downward at an angle of about thirty degrees, and he found he could hear the voices more clearly when his left ear was pressed against the shaft.

Abruptly he sat up, pulling himself roughly onto his knees. Clearing away as much of the loose masonry as he could, he examined the shaft, pressing his ear against it.

In the majority of positions he could hear nothing, but, by some acoustical freak, in a small area of a few square inches the voices were clearly magnified. Obviously the ventilator shaft, now disused, led down into the station only a few yards below, and was reflecting the voices of the doctors moving about their patients, particularly a burnt power-station worker whose cot was directly below the mouth of the shaft.

The galvanized iron plating was only an eighth of an inch thick, but there was nothing in the rubble around him which he could use to cut it. He pounded on it with his fists, shouted against it, pressing his ear to the focal area to hear any answering call. He banged it tirelessly with a brick, to no avail.

Finally he picked up the torch, carefully selected the focal area and began to tap patiently with it, whenever he heard the doctors below, the 'shave-and-a-haircut, shampoo' rhythm of childhood.

Two hours later, several eternities after the battery had exhausted itself, he heard an answering shout below.

After six o'clock the lounge would begin to fill. One of the stewards behind the bar switched on the phonograph and turned up the recessed lighting, masking the thin cream-and-chartreuse paint on the fresh concrete, and so the transformation of a recreation bunker 150 feet below USAF Brandon Hall into a Mayfair cocktail lounge would be acceptably complete.

Donald Maitland never ceased to wonder at the effectiveness of the illusion. Here at least was a small oasis of illusion.

Beyond the lounge, with its chromium bar and red leather, its tinsel and plastic lighting, were service sections as bleak as anything in the Seigfried Line, but as the uniformed officers and their wives and the senior civilians began to make their way in there was little hint of the 350 mph gales at present ravaging the world.

His five days at Brandon Hall he had largely spent in the recreation lounge. Fortunately his injuries at Knightsbridge were comparatively minor, and half an hour from now, at 6.30 p.m., he would officially report for duty again.

He watched Charles Avery carry their drinks over to the table, and stirred himself pleasantly. Americans were expert at providing the civilized amenities of life with a minimum of apparent effort or pomp, and in his five days at Brandon Hall he had begun to forget Susan's tragic death and its implied judgement on himself.

'Up to three-fifty,' Avery remarked sombrely, trying to straighten the creases in his black battledress jacket with its surgeon's insignia. 'There's damn little left up there now. How do you feel?'

Maitland shrugged, listening to the low rhythm of a foxtrot he had last heard years earlier when he had taken Susan out to the Milroy. 'O.K. I wouldn't exactly say I was eager to get back into action, but I'm ready enough. It's been pleasant down here. These five days have given me my first real chance in years to see myself calmly. Pity I've got to leave.'

Avery nodded. 'Frankly, I wouldn't bother. There's little you'll be able to do to help. The Americans are still sending out a few vehicles, but in general everything's closing down. Contact between separate units seems pretty limited and outside news is coming through very slowly.'

'How's London holding out?'

Avery shook his head, peered into his glass. 'London? It doesn't exist. No more than New York, or Tokyo or Moscow. The TV monitor tower at Hammersmith just shows a sea of rubble. There's not a single building standing.'

'It's amazing casualties are so light.'

'I don't know whether they are. My guess is that half a million people in London have been killed. As far as Tokyo or Bombay are concerned it's anybody's guess. At least fifty per cent, I should think. There's a simple physical limit to how long an individual can stand up to a 350-mile-an-hour air stream. Thank God for the Underground system.'

Maitland echoed this. After his rescue at Knightsbridge he had been astounded by the efficient organization that existed below street level, a sub-world of dark labyrinthine tunnels and shafts crowded with countless thousands of almost motionless beings, huddled together on the unlit platforms with their drab bundles of possessions, waiting patiently for the wind to subside, like the denizens of some vast gallery of the dead waiting for their resurrection.

Where the others were Maitland could only guess. A fortunate aspect of the overcrowding of most major cities and metropolitan complexes around the world was that expansion had forced construction to take place not only upward and outward, but downward as well. Thousands of inverted buildings hung from street level – car parks, underground cinemas, sub-basements and sub-sub-basements – which now provided tolerable shelter, sealed off from the ravaging wind by the collapsing structures above. Millions more must be clinging to life in these readymade bunkers, sandwiched in narrow angles between concrete ledges, their ears deafened by the roar above, completely out of contact with everyone else.

What would happen when their supplies of food began to run out?

'Six-fifteen, Donald,' Avery cut in. He finished his drink and sat forward, ready to leave. 'I'm working at Casualty Intake from now on. The Americans are shipping most of their top brass over to their bases in Greenland – the wind's about fifty miles an hour lower than here. Rumour has it

142

that they're converting some big underground ICBM shelters inside the Arctic Circle, and with luck a few useful Nato personnel may be invited along to do the rough work. From now on I'm going to keep my eyes open for some amenable two-star general with a sprained ankle to whom I can make myself indispensable as back-scratcher and house-boy. I advise you to do the same.'

Maitland turned and looked curiously at Avery, was surprised to see that the surgeon was perfectly serious. 'I admire your shrewdness,' he said quietly. 'But I hope we can look after ourselves if we have to.'

'Well, we can't,' Avery scoffed. 'Let's face it, we haven't really done so for a long time. I know it sounds despicable, but adaptability is the only real biological qualification for survival. At the moment a pretty grim form of natural selection is taking place, and frankly I want to be selected. Sneer at me if you wish – I willingly concede you that posthumous right.' He paused for a moment, waiting for Maitland to reply, but the latter sat staring bleakly into his glass and Avery asked: 'By the way, heard anything of Andrew Symington?'

'As far as I know he's still with Marshall's intelligence unit over at Whitehall. Dora's just had her baby; I mean to look in on her before I leave.'

As they made their way out of the lounge, they passed a tall American submarine commander who had come in with a slim blonde-haired girl in a brown uniform with Press tabs on its sleeves. Her face and neck were covered with minute abrasions, the typical wind-exposure scars, but she seemed so relaxed, following the American closely with unforced intimacy, that he realized these two, who had obviously come through a period of prolonged exposure together, were the first people he had seen who had managed to preserve their own private world intact.

As he took his seat in the briefing room in the Personnel Reallocation Unit he wondered how far his own character had benefited by the ordeals he had been through, how much it had gained merit, as the Buddhists would say. Could he really claim any moral superiority over Avery, for example? Despite his near death at Knightsbridge he had so far had little choice in determining his own fate. Events had driven him forward at their own pace. How would he behave when he was given a choice?

Maitland was assigned to one of the big Titan super-tractors ferrying VIP's and embassy personnel down to the submarine base at Portsmouth. Many of the passengers would be suffering from major injuries sustained before their rescue, and required careful supervision.

Listening to the briefing, Maitland had the impression, as Avery had suggested, that the Americans were withdrawing in considerable numbers, taking with them even severe surgical cases. When the last convoy had set sail for Greenland, would Brandon Hall have outlived its usefulness? The nearest British base was at Biggin Hill, and if the wind continued to rise for the next week or so it would be difficult to reach. Besides, what sort of welcome would they receive if they did go there?

The captain confirmed his doubts.

'How far is there any effective contact between the bases around London?' Maitland asked as the meeting broke up. 'I feel we're all pulling the lids down over our respective holes and sealing them tight.'

The captain nodded sombrely. 'That's just about it. God knows what's going to happen when they decide to close this place. It's cosy down here now, but we're on board a sinking ship. There's only about one week's supply of generator fuel left in the storage tanks, and when that's gone it's going to get damned chilly. And when the pumps stop we'll have to climb into our diving suits. The caissons below the foundations have shifted and water's pouring in from underground wells. At present we're pumping it out at the rate of about a thousand gallons an hour.'

Maitland collected his kitbag from the hospital dormitory. On the way out he looked in at the women's ward, and went over to Dora Symington's cubicle.

'Hullo, Donald,' Dora greeted him. She managed a brave smile, made a space for him on the bed among the feeding bottles and milk cans. She raised the baby's head. 'I've been telling him he looks like Andrew, but I'm not sure he agrees. What do you think?'

Maitland considered the baby's small wizened face. He would have liked to think it symbolized hope and courage, the new world being reborn unknown to them in the cataclysmic midst of the old, but in fact he felt grimly depressed. Dora's courage, her pathetic little cubicle with its makeshift shelves and clutter of damp clothes, made him realize just how helpless they were, how near the centre of the whirlpool.

'Have you heard from Andrew yet?' she asked, bringing the question out carefully.

'No, but don't worry, Dora. He's in the best possible company. Marshall knows how to look after himself.'

He talked to her for a few minutes and then excused himself, taking one of the elevators up to the transport pool three levels below the surface.

Even here, some seventy-five feet below ground, separated by enormous concrete shields ten feet thick, designed to provide protection at ground zero against megaton nuclear weapons, the presence of the storm wind raging above was immediately apparent. Despite the giant airlocks and overlaying ramps the narrow corridors were thick with black sandy grit forced in under tremendous pressure, the air damp and cold as the air stream carried with it enormous quantities of water vapour – in some cases the contents of entire seas, such as the Caspian and the Great Lakes, which had been drained dry, their beds plainly visible.

Drivers and surface personnel, all sealed into heavy plastic suits, thick foam padding puffing up their bodies, hung about between the half-dozen Titan super-tractors grouped around the service station.

His own Titan was the fifth in line, a giant six-tracked articulated crawler with steeply raked sides and profile, over eighty feet long and twenty feet wide, the tracks six feet broad. The grey-painted sides of the vehicle had been slashed and pitted, the heavy three-inch steel plate scarred with deep dents where flying rocks and masonry had struck the vehicle, almost completely obliterating the US Navy insignia painted along the hull.

A lean-faced big-shouldered man in a blue surface suit looked up from a discussion with two mechanics who were sitting inside one of the tracks, adjusting the massive cleats. Royal Canadian Navy tabs were clipped to his collar, a captain's rank bars.

'Dr Maitland?' he asked in a deep pleasant voice. When Maitland nodded he put out his hand and shook Maitland's warmly in a powerful grip. 'Good to have you aboard. My name's Jim Halliday. Welcome to the Toronto Belle.' He jerked a thumb at the Titan. 'We've got just over half an hour before we take off, so how about some coffee?'

'Good idea,' Maitland agreed. Halliday took the canvas grip out of his hand, to his surprise walked around to the front of the tractor and slung it up over the hood onto the driver's hatchway. As Halliday rejoined him, Maitland said: 'I was going to leave the grip in the mess in case we have to make a quick getaway.'

Halliday shook his head, taking Maitland's arm. 'If you want to, Doc, go ahead. Frankly, I recommend that you make yourself at home aboard the ship. Can't say I feel any too confident about this place.'

As they collected their coffee in the canteen and sat down at the end of one of the long wooden tables Maitland examined Halliday's face carefully. The Canadian looked solid and resourceful, unlikely to be swayed by rumour.

They exchanged personal histories briefly. By now, Maitland noticed, there were so many disaster stories, so many confirmed and unconfirmed episodes of heroism, such a confusion of dramatic and tragic events that those still surviving confined themselves to the barest self-identification. In addition, there was the gradual numbness that had begun to affect everyone, a blunting of the sensibilities, by the filth and privation and sheer buffeting momentum of the wind. The result was an increasing concentration on ensuring one's own personal survival, a reluctance, such as he had just seen in a basically confident man like Halliday, to put any trust in the durability of others.

'Our last trip we carried only three passengers,' Halliday explained, 'so a medic wasn't needed. It's obvious they'll soon be closing the unit down.'

Maitland nodded. 'What will happen to us then?'

Halliday glanced up at him briefly, then flung his cigarette butt into the coffee dregs. 'I'll leave you to guess. Frankly, we rate a pretty low order of importance. As long as movement above surface is possible, the big tractors have a valuable role, but now – well. . . . Just about all the VIPs have got where they want to be; the perimeter's really being pulled in tight. Have you been up top recently?'

'Not for about a week,' Maitland admitted.

'It's hard to describe – pretty rough. Solid roaring wall of black air – except that it's not air any more but a horizontal avalanche of dust and rock, like sitting right behind a jet engine full on with the exhaust straight in your face. Can't see where the hell you're going, landmarks obliterated, roads buried under tons of rubble. We steer by the beam transmitted between here and Portsmouth. When the stations close down our job will be over. Only yesterday we lost one of the big rigs – their radio broke down when they were somewhere south of Leatherhead. They tried to make it back by compass and drove straight into the river.'

As they neared the tractor Maitland saw a small group of passengers waiting, two men and a young woman. All the hatches were being secured on the rear section of the vehicle, and it looked as if these three were the full complement and would travel in the forward section, leaving the rear empty. As Halliday had said, it seemed a complete waste of fuel and personnel – the Titan would have been better employed rescuing Andrew Symington and Marshall – and Maitland felt a sudden sensation of resentment towards the three passengers.

One was a small plum-faced man with a brush moustache, the other two a tall American in a navy trench coat and the girl wearing a leather helmet, goggles over her forehead. As he approached she slipped her hand under the American's arm, and he recognized the couple who had passed him in the lounge bar.

Halliday gestured Maitland over, introduced him briefly to the passengers. 'Commander Lanyon, this is Dr Maitland. He'll be riding down to Portsmouth with us. If you want your temperature taken, Miss Olsen, just ask him.'

Maitland nodded to the trio and helped the young woman, an NBC television reporter, carrying her tape recorder over to the starboard hatchway. She and Commander Lanyon had just reached England from the Mediterranean, had come up to London with the third member of the group, an Associated Press correspondent called Waring, in the hope of getting material for their networks back in the States. Unfortunately their hopes that the wind would have subsided had not been fulfilled, and they were returning empty-handed, en route for Greenland.

Ten minutes later the seven of them – three passengers, Maitland, Halliday, the driver and radio operator – were sealed down into the forward section of the Titan, a narrow compartment fifteen feet long by six feet wide, packed with equipment, stores and miscellaneous baggage. Canvas racks folded down from the sides and Maitland and the passengers sat cramped together on these, the three crew members up forward, Halliday at the periscope immediately behind the driver, the radio operator beside him. A single light behind a grille on the ceiling cast a thin glow over the compartment, fading and brightening as the engines varied in speed.

For half an hour they hardly moved, edging forward or backward a few yards in answer to instructions transmitted over the R/T. The roar of the engines precluded any but the most rudimentary conversation between those at the back, and Maitland let himself sink off into a mindless reverie, interrupted by sudden jolts that woke him back to an uneasy reality.

Finally they began to move forward, the engines surging below them, and at the same time the vehicle tilted backward sharply, at an angle of over ten degrees, as they climbed the exit ramp.

The air in the tractor became suddenly cooler, as if a powerful refrigerating unit had been switched on in the compartment. They appeared to be moving along a tunnel carved through an iceberg, and Maitland remembered someone at the base telling him that the surface air temperature was now falling by a full degree per day. The air stream moving over the oceans was forcing an enormous uptake of water by evaporation, and consequently cooling the surfaces below.

The Titan levelled off on the final exit shelf, then laboured slowly up the last incline.

Immediately, as the huge vehicle slewed about unsteadily, its tracks searching for equilibrium in the ragged surface, the familiar tattoo of thousands of flying missiles rattled across the sides and roof around them like endless salvos of machine-gun fire. The noise was enervating, occasionally appearing to slacken off slightly, then resuming with even greater force as a cloud of higher-density particles drove across them.

Standing behind the driver, Halliday steered the Titan by looking through the periscope. Occasionally, when they moved across open country, he left the driver to follow the compass bearing provided by the radio operator, and came back to the passengers, crouching down to exchange a few words.

'We're just passing through Biggin Hill,' he told them after they had been under way for half an hour. 'Used to be an RAF base here, but it was flooded out after the east wall of the main shelter collapsed. About five hundred people were trapped inside; only six got away.'

'Can I take a look outside, Captain?' Patricia Olsen asked. 'I've been underground so long I feel like a mole.'

'Surely,' Halliday agreed. 'Not that there's a damn thing to see.'

They all moved forward, swaying from side to side like strap-hangers on a rocking Underground train as the tractor slid and dragged under the impact of the wind.

Maitland waited until Lanyon and Patricia had finished, then pressed his eyes to the binocular viewpiece.

Sweeping the periscope around, he saw that they were moving along the remains of the M5 Motorway down to Portsmouth.

Little of the road was still intact. The soft shoulders and grass centre pieces between the lanes had disappeared, leaving in their place a four-foot-deep hollow trough. Here and there the stump of a concrete telegraph pole protruded from the verge, or a battered overpass, huge pieces chipped from its arches, spanned the roadway, but otherwise the landscape was completely blighted. Occasionally a dark shadow would flash by, the remains of some airborne structure – aircraft fusilage or motor car – bouncing and cartwheeling along the ground.

Maitland leaned against the periscope mounting. With the topsoil gone, and the root-system which held the surface together and provided a secure foothold for arable crops against the erosive forces of rain and wind, the entire surface of the globe would dust bowl in the way that the

Oklahoma farmland had literally disappeared into the air in the 1920s.

As he turned away from the periscope, Halliday was right beside the radio operator. A signal was coming through from Brandon Hall, and the operator took off his headphones and passed them to the captain.

'Bad news, Doctor,' the operator said. 'Flash in from Brandon Hall about a friend of yours, Andrew Symington. Apparently the emergency intelligence unit in the Admiralty bunkers were attacked yesterday. Marshall and three of the others were shot.'

Maitland gripped the strap over his head. 'Andrew? Is he dead?'

'No, they don't think so. His body hasn't been found, anyway. Marshall managed to get an alert through before he died. The gunmen were working for someone called Hardoon. As far as I could make out he's supposed to have a private army operating from a secret base somewhere in the Guildford area.'

'I've run into Hardoon before,' Maitland cut in. 'Marshall was also working for him.' Quickly he recounted his discovery of the crates of paramilitary equipment in Marshall's warehouse, the uniformed guards. 'Hardoon must have decided to get rid of Marshall; probably he'd outlived his usefulness.' He looked up at the strap in his hand, and jerked it roughly. 'What the hell could have happened to Symington, though?'

Halliday lowered his head doubtfully. 'Well, maybe he's O.K.' he said, managing a show of sympathy. 'It's hard to say.'

'Don't worry,' Maitland said confidently. 'Symington's a top electronics and communications man, far more valuable to Hardoon now than a TV mogul like Marshall. If his body wasn't found in the bunker he must still be alive. Hardoon's men wouldn't waste time carrying a corpse around.' He paused, listening to the hail drive across the

151

roof. 'All those crates were labelled "Hardoon Tower." This secret base must be there.'

Halliday shook his head. 'Never heard of it. Though the name Hardoon is familiar. What is he, a political big shot?'

'Shipping and hotel magnate,' Maitland told him. 'Something of a power-crazy eccentric. "Hardoon Tower" – God knows where, though.'

'Sounds like a hotel,' Halliday commented. 'If it is, it won't be standing, that's for sure. Sorry about your friend, but as you say, he'll probably be O.K. there.'

Maitland nodded, leaning on the radio set and searching his mind for where Hardoon Tower might be. He noticed the radio operator watching him pensively, was about to turn away and rejoin the trio at the rear of the compartment when the man said:

'The Hardoon place is just near here, sir. About ten miles away, at Leatherhead.'

Maitland turned back. 'Are you sure?'

'Well, I can't be certain,' the operator said. 'But we get a lot of interference from a station operating from Leatherhead. It's using a scrambled vhf beam, definitely not a government installation.'

'Could be anyone, though,' Maitland said. 'Weather station, police unit, some VIP outfit.'

The operator shook his head. 'I don't think so, sir. They were trying to identify it back at Brandon Hall; there was even an M15 signals expert there. I heard him refer to Hardoon.'

Maitland turned to Halliday. 'What about it, Captain? He's probably right. We could make a small detour out to Leatherhead.'

Halliday shook his head curtly. 'Sorry, Maitland. I'd like to, but our reserve tank only holds two hundred gallons, barely enough to get us back.'

'Then what about uncoupling the rear section?' Maitland asked. 'It's no damn use anyway.'

'Maybe not. But what are we supposed to do, even if we find this character Hardoon? Put him under arrest?'

Halliday returned to the periscope, indicating that their argument was closed, and hunched over the eyepiece, scanning the road. Maitland stood behind him, undecided, watching the radio-compass beam on the navigator's screen. They followed the beam carefully, driving along a razor edge between a stream of dots – leftward error – and a stream of dashes – rightward error. At present they were deliberately three degrees off course, in order to take advantage of the motorway's firm foundations. Halliday was following a bend in the road, and the radio compass rotated steadily, from 145 degrees to 150 degrees, and then on around to 160 degrees. Unoccupied for the moment, the operator was searching the waveband of the vhf set. He picked up a blurred staccato signal and gestured to Maitland.

'That's the Hardoon signal, sir.'

Maitland nodded. He stepped over to the operator as if to hear the scrambled signal more clearly, and slowly eased his torch out of his hip pocket, clasping the heavy cylinder with its steel-encased reflector firmly in his right hand. He edged between the operator and the compass, which was still revolving. When he was satisfied that the operator would no longer remember the precise bearing, he raised the torch and with a quick backhand stroke tapped in the glass screen.

Quickly he began to hammer away at the set, smashing in the compass and plunging the torch into the valve-crammed cabinet. Shouting to Halliday, the operator struggled to his feet and tried to pull Maitland away. Then Halliday swung back from the periscope and flung his arms around Maitland's shoulders. The three men wrestled together, their blows muffled by the swaying vehicle and their heavy clothing, then fell to the floor.

As they struggled onto their knees, the tractor, still following the circular course Halliday had been giving to the driver, tipped over sharply as it left the roadway and ran rapidly down the incline.

Halliday pulled Maitland to his feet, his face thick with anger. Lanyon had joined them, and helped the radio operator to rise. The corporal stumbled over to the set and stared blankly at the wrecked console, his fingers numbly tracing the ragged outlines of the compass.

He looked wildly at Halliday. 'The set's a write-off, captain, a total wreck! God knows what our bearing was! We were moving around that bend. I wasn't watching it.'

Halliday wrenched at Maitland's jacket. 'You damn fool! Do you realize we're completely lost?'

Maitland shook himself free. 'No you're not, Captain. I hate to force your hand, but it was the only way. Look.'

He reached across to the vhf set and turned up the volume, so that the staccato gabble of the mysterious station sounded out into the compartment over the noise of the wind beating against the tractor. With one hand he rotated the set in its bearings until, at an angle of 45 degrees to the lateral axis of the tractor, it was at maximum strength.

'Our new direction beam. Follow that and it should take us straight to Hardoon Tower.'

'How can you be sure?' Halliday snapped. 'It could be anything!'

Maitland shrugged. 'Maybe, but it's our only chance.' He turned to Lanyon, quickly explained what had happened to Andrew Symington.

Lanyon pondered this for a few minutes, then turned to Halliday, who was peering through the periscope.

'Seems as if we've no alternative, Captain. As it's only a few miles away, a short detour won't hurt us. And there's always the chance that if this fellow Hardoon is planning some sort of take-over when the wind blows out, we may be able to anticipate him.'

Halliday clenched his fists, scowling angrily, then nodded and swung back to the periscope.

Five minutes later they reversed onto the highway and moved off down a side road towards Leatherhead, following the vhf signal. Maitland had expected that they would have difficulty in locating Hardoon Tower, but Halliday soon noticed something that confirmed his suspicions about Hardoon.

'Take a look for yourself,' Halliday said. 'This road has been used regularly all through the last four or five weeks. There's even wire mesh laid down at the exposed corners.'

Lanyon took the periscope, confirmed this with a nod. 'Heavy tracked vehicles,' he commented. 'Must have been carrying some really big loads.' Grinning, he added: 'Looks as if Pat may get a story after all.'

They followed the signal, steadily increasing in strength, towards the Hardoon estates at Leatherhead, as much guided by signs of recent activity along the road as by the radio beam, the wind pushing them on at a steady 25 mph.

Two hours later they had their first sight of Hardoon Tower.

Maitland was doing his fifteen-minute turn at the periscope when the operator told him that they had entered the zone of maximum signal strength.

'Could be anywhere within a couple of square miles of here,' he reported, swinging the direction-finder aerial without influencing the volume. 'From now on we'll have to make visual contact.'

Maitland peered through the periscope. Ahead the roadway had broadened into a furrowed band of shattered concrete and wire mesh about 100 yards wide, stained with huge white and grey patches which suggested some enormous roadwork had recently been in progress. The tractor edged forward along the centre at 15 mph, tacking from left to right across the band. Two hundred yards away the road disappeared into the dim whirling mass of the wind stream. Beside the roadway the ground was black and dark, devoid of all vegetation, dotted with a few huge rolling objects, stumps of giant trees, blocks of masonry, all moving from left to right across their path.

Ahead, high in the air, something loomed for a moment, a lighter patch of sky, apparently an interval in the dust cloud. Maitland ignored it, searching the ground carefully for any hidden side turning.

A few seconds later he realized that the strip of lighter air was still in front of him.

Straight ahead, its massive bulk veiled by the dust-storm, an enormous pyramid-like structure reared up, its four-angled sides 100 feet across at the base, tapering to the apex eighty feet above. The tractor was now about a quarter of a mile away and, although partly obscured, the pyramid was the first structure Maitland had seen for weeks which retained hard clean outlines. Even at this distance he could see its straight profiles, the perfectly pointed apex, cleaving the dark air stream like the prow of a liner.

He gestured Halliday over to the periscope. As the captain whooped in surprise, Maitland gestured to Lanyon.

'It looks as if Hardoon's strongpoint is up ahead. About three or four hundred yards away. A huge concrete pyramid.'

'It's fantastic,' Halliday said over his shoulder, centring the periscope. 'Who does the maniac think he is – Cheops? Must have taken years to build.'

He handed over the periscope to Lanyon, who nodded slowly. 'Either years or thousands of men. The roadways indicate there's been a pretty big construction force on the job.'

They edged nearer the pyramid, its great bulk rising above into the flickering sky. Two hundred yards away the tractor struck a low obstacle with its offside front track, and they looked down at a low wall, ten feet high, rising out of the ground and running in the direction of the left-hand corner of the pyramid. The wall was ten feet wide, a massive reinforced concrete buttress. As they moved along it, a second rampart appeared out of the gravel-like soil on their right, and they found themselves entering a long approach system of parallel concrete walls, partly intended as wind-breakers for the pyramid, and partly to screen entering vehicles.

Maitland searched the face of the pyramid for apertures, but its surface was smooth and unbroken. Gradually as the height of the supporting walls increased, it was lost from sight and they entered a narrow ramp that led below an overhanging shoulder and then around a right-angle corner into what appeared to be a dead end.

Halliday tilted back the periscope, craning to look up at the great bulk of the pyramid obscured by the stream of dust and gravel cascading across its surface.

'Looks as if this isn't an approach road after all,' Halliday commented. 'No entrance bays or locks. We'll have one hell of a job reversing out of here. Why don't they put up some signs?'

Suddenly they swayed on their feet, grabbed at the ceiling straps. The tractor had dropped abruptly, was moving steadily downward like an elevator.

Maitland dived for the periscope, just in time to see the walls around them soar upward into the air, the apex of the pyramid disappear. Seconds later the rectangular outlines of an elevator opening rose above them. The black sides of the shaft ran past, then slowed down as the elevator reached its floor. A horizontal lock slid across the opening and sealed it, shutting out the daylight.

'Well, they must be friendly,' Halliday decided. 'I was beginning to wonder how we'd get in if they didn't want us.'

The driver cut the engines, and as the din subsided they

heard mechanics outside the tractor shackling exit ladders to its turret. Halliday began to unlock the hatchway, motioned to the others to get to their feet.

'Stretch your legs, everybody. May be our last chance for days.'

He opened the hatch, raising it a few inches, and someone on the roof pulled it back. He climbed out, followed by Maitland and the radio operator.

The tractor was at the bottom of a large freight-elevator shaft, part of an underground bunker from which high driveways led off to dark transport bays. Men in black plastic suits and helmets stood around the tractor, most of them with holsters on their belts. Maitland recognized the uniforms he had seen in Marshall's Park Lane basement.

As he swung down, a tall, rough-featured man with a white pyramid-shaped triangle on the front of his helmet stepped over to him.

'What are you clowns playing at?' he snapped. 'Why the hell aren't you using your radio?'

His voice was a snarl of irritation and violence. He looked at Maitland, then grabbed him in surprise, glancing up at Halliday, who was helping the radio operator out of the turret.

'What's all this?' the big man snapped. He wrenched Maitland around roughly, fingering his navy weather jacket. 'Where's Kroll? He was supposed to bring Symington. Who are all you people?'

'Isn't Symington here?' Maitland asked him.

The big man stared at him angrily, then looked over his shoulder and gestured towards a squad of guards who were encircling the tractor. At the same time he reached for his holster.

Halliday was still standing on the roof, gesturing back the radio operator, who was about to join Maitland on the ground.

The squad of black-suited guards closed in around the

Titan, two or three of them swarming up its sides. Maitland found himself seized by the neck, jabbed an elbow into his attacker and fell backward with him against one of the tracks. He kicked himself loose from the man and struck out at two others who closed in on him, butting them with his head. One of them punched him hard in the face, the other grabbed him around the waist and pulled him downward onto the ground again. As he lay there struggling he saw the big guard backing away from the tractor, a heavy .45 automatic in his hand. Everyone seemed to be shouting, and then the .45 roared out twice, the flashes from its barrel lighting up the sides of the Titan.

A figure, apparently Halliday, came lurching down the ladder, stumbled a few feet across the floor and then fell onto its face.

Maitland slammed a fist into the back of one of the men lying across him, managed to free himself for a moment. He was trying to sit forward, when someone ran up and kicked him heavily in the side of the head.

His brain exploding like a roman candle, he fell backward into a deep roaring pool of darkness.

Chapter 8

The Tower of Hardoon

As he woke his head was swinging like a piston from side to to side.

A dozen arteries pounded angrily inside his skull, rivers of thudding pain. He opened his eyes and focused them with an effort. A powerfully-built guard in a black plastic uniform, a large white triangle on his helmet, was leaning over him, slapping his face with a broad open hand.

When he saw Maitland's eyes were open, he gave him a final vicious backhand cut, then snapped at the two guards holding Maitland in his chair. They jerked him forward into a sitting position, then let go of his hands.

Gasping for air, Maitland tried to control himself, spread his legs apart and pressed his shoulders against the stiff backrest of the chair. Above, fluorescent lighting shone across a low bare ceiling. In a few seconds his face had stopped stinging, and he lowered his eyes slowly.

Directly in front of him, across a wide crocodile-skin desk, sat a squat, broad-shouldered man in a dark suit. His head was huge and bull-like; below a high domed forehead were two small eyes, a short stump of nose, a mouth like a scar, and a jutting chin. The expression was sombre and menacing.

He surveyed Maitland coldly, ignoring the red-flecked saliva Maitland was wiping away from his bruised lips. Dimly, Maitland recognized a face he had seen in a few rare magazine photographs. This, he realized, was Hardoon. Wondering how long had elapsed since their arrival, Maitland began to glance around the room. He was aware of

Hardoon sitting forward and tapping his knuckles on the desk.

'Are you completely with us again, Doctor?' he asked, his voice soft yet callous. He waited for Maitland to murmur, then nodded to the guards, who took up their positions against the rear wall.

'Good. While you were resting your companions have been telling me about your exploit. I'm sorry that your little outing has ended here. I must apologize for the stupidity of my traffic police. They should never have allowed you in. Unfortunately, Kroll –' he indicated the tall guard with the single helmet triangle, lounging against the wall beside the desk '– was somewhat delayed on his return, or you would have been able to continue your journey to Portsmouth unmolested.'

He examined Maitland for a moment taking a cigar from a silver ashtray on the pedestal behind the desk.

Puzzled why Hardoon was bothering to interrogate him, Maitland massaged his face, peering around the room.

He was in a large oak-panelled office, the heavy walls of which appeared to be completely solid, flatly absorbing the sounds of their voices. Behind him, where the guards stood, were high bookshelves, divided by a doorway. There were no windows, but on the far side of Hardoon's desk was a shoulder-high alcove sealed by high shutters.

Hardoon drew reflectively on his cigar. 'I gather that once again I am persona non grata with the authorities.' he went on in his slow leisurely voice. 'It was foolish of Kroll to allow Marshall to broadcast our whereabouts to all and sundry. However, that is another matter.'

Maitland sat forward, aware of the guards poised on their toes behind him, the huge figure of Kroll stiffening slightly. 'What happened to Halliday?' he asked, tongue tripping inside his bruised mouth. 'He was shot as we arrived.'

Hardoon's face was blank, his eyes narrowing as he considered the interruption. 'A tragic misunderstanding.

Believe me, Doctor, I abhor violence as much as you. My traffic police assumed that you were Kroll. Your vehicles are of the same type, with identical markings. When they discovered their mistake they were naturally rather excited. These accidents happen.'

His tone was matter-of-fact, but even though his eyes were fixed coldly on Maitland's face the latter had the distinct impression that most of Hardoon's attention was elsewhere. His voice seemed to be an agent that was automatically carrying out instructions given to it previously, like the guards standing behind Maitland.

'Where are the others?' Maitland asked. 'The two Americans and the girl?'

Hardoon gestured with his cigar. 'In the –' he searched for a suitable phrase '– visitors' quarters. They are perfectly comfortable. Mr Symington was slightly injured en route, and is now resting in the sick bay. A useful man; let us hope he is soon recovered.'

Maitland studied Hardoon's face. The millionaire was about fifty-five, still physically powerful, but with curious lustreless eyes. Despite its hard edge, his voice almost droned.

'Now, Doctor, to come to the point. The arrival here of you and your three companions presents me with an opportunity I have decided to make the most of.' As Maitland frowned, Hardoon smiled deprecatingly. 'No, I am not in need of medical attention; far from it. We have an ample number of doctors and nurses here. In fact, you will find this one of the most efficiently organized bastions against the wind in existence, if not *the* most efficient, my traffic police notwithstanding.'

He pressed a button set into a small control panel on the desk in front of him, and then turned slightly in his chair to face the shutters, gesturing Maitland to do the same. The shutters began to retract. Behind Maitland the ceiling lights dimmed, and as the shutters slid into their housings they revealed an enormous block of plate glass, three feet deep and twice as wide, apparently set into the face of the pyramid.

Sloping away below was the east wall of the pyramid. At its base were the causeways and entrance passage they had taken to the elevator. Beyond, obscured by the storm, was the wide approach road. The wind stream swept directly towards them, the thousands of fragments carried past at incredible speeds, vaulting out of the lowering storm cloud on a thousand trajectories.

At the same time Hardoon had pressed another tab on the desk, and a loudspeaker on the wall above the window crackled into life. Muted at first, and then rising to full volume, was the bare, unalloyed voice of the wind stream, the roaring Niagara of sound that had pursued Maitland in his nightmares for the past month.

Hardoon sat back, watching the wind through the window, listening to it on the speaker. He seemed to sink into some private reverie, his cigar half raised to his lips, its smoke curling away towards a ventilator in the ceiling. An automatic rheostat must have been mounted to the speaker, for the volume rose steadily, until the noise of the storm wind filled the office, a blast of rushing air like the sounds of an experimental wind tunnel at maximum velocity.

Suddenly Hardoon woke out of his trance and stabbed the two buttons. The sound abruptly fell away, and the shutters glided back and locked across the window.

For a moment Hardoon stared at the darkened panels. 'Its force is incredible,' he commented to Maitland. 'Nature herself in revolt, in her purest, most elemental form. And where is Man, her prime enemy? For the most part vanquished, utterly defeated, hiding below ground like a terror-stricken mole, or wandering about blindly down dark tunnels.'

He looked at Maitland rhetorically, then added: 'I admire you, Doctor, and your companions. You still do battle with the wind, to some extent retain your initiative. You move about the surface of the globe undeterred. I'm sorry that Captain Halliday should have been killed.'

Maitland nodded. His head had finally cleared, the warmth of the office reviving him. He decided to take the initiative in their conversation, and sat forward. 'When did you start building this pyramid?' he asked.

Hardoon shrugged. 'Years ago. The bunkers were originally designed as my personal shelter in the event of World War III, but the pyramid was completed only this month.'

Maitland pressed on. 'What are you hoping to gain? Supreme political control when the wind subsides?'

Hardoon turned and stared at Maitland, an expression of incredulity on his face.

'Is that what occurs to you, Doctor? You can think of no other motive?'

Maitland shrugged, somewhat taken aback by Hardoon's reaction. 'Your own immediate survival, of course. With the backing of a large, well-run organization.'

Hardoon smiled bleakly. 'It's astonishing, how the weak always judge the strong by their own limited standards. It's precisely for this reason that you're here.' Before Maitland could ask him to expand upon this he said: 'Surely the unusual design of this shelter indicates my real motives. In fact, up to now I assumed this was the case. It must be obvious that if survival and the maintenance of a powerful and well-equipped private army were my object I would certainly not choose to house myself in an exposed pyramid.'

'It is a vantage point,' Maitland pointed out. 'As you've just demonstrated, it makes an excellent observation post.'

'To observe what? That window is only sixty feet above ground. What could I hope to see?'

'Nothing, I suppose. Except the wind.'

Hardoon bowed his head slightly. 'Doctor, you are entirely correct. The wind is, indeed, all I wish to see from here. And at the same time I intend it to see me.' He paused, then went on. 'As the wind has risen so everyone on the globe has built downward, trying to escape it; has burrowed further and deeper into the shelter of the earth's mantle. With one exception – myself. I alone have built upward, have dared to challenge the wind, asserting Man's courage and determination to master nature. If I were to claim political power – which, most absolutely, I will not – I would do so simply on the basis of my own moral superiority. Only I, in the face of the greatest holocaust ever to strike the earth, have had the moral courage to attempt to outstare nature. That is my sole reason for building this tower. Here on the surface of the globe I meet nature on her own terms, in the arena of her choice. If I fail, Man has no right to assert his innate superiority over the unreason of the natural world.'

Maitland nodded, watching Hardoon closely. The millionaire had spoken in a quiet clipped voice, using neither gesture nor emphasis. He realized that Hardoon was almost certainly sincere, and wondered to himself whether this made him less or more dangerous. How much was he prepared to sacrifice to put his philosophy to the test?

'Well, if what you say is true, it's a spectacular gesture. But surely there are equal challenges to one's moral courage in everyday life?'

'For you, perhaps. But my talents and position force me to play my role on a larger stage. You probably think me an insane megalomaniac. How else, though, can I demonstrate my moral courage? As an industrialist, moral courage is less important than judgement and experience. What should I do? Found a university, endow a thousand scholarships, give away my money to the poor? But a single signature on a cheque will do these for me, and I know that with my talents I will never be destitute. Fly to the moon? I'm too old. Face bravely the prospect of my own death? But my health is still sound. There is nothing, no other way in which I can prove myself.'

Maitland found himself smiling. 'In that case, I can only wish you luck. As you've said, this is a private duel between yourself and the wind. So you'll have no objections to our collecting Symington and going on our way.'

Hardoon raised a hand. 'Unfortunately, I do, Doctor. Why do you think I've brought you up here? Now, I think, you understand my real motives, but did you even five minutes ago? I doubt it. In fact, you thought I was avid for political power and taking advantage of my industrial interests to seize a defenceless world. And so will everybody else. Not that it matters particularly, but I would like my stand here to serve as an example to others faced with similar challenges in the future. I claim no credit for any courage I show, and any due to me I gladly pass on to homo sapiens, my brother-at-large.' Hardoon gestured with his cigar. 'Now, by a stroke of fortune two of your companions are newspaper reporters, both highly placed members of their profession. Given the right frame of mind, the right perspective, they might well prepare an accurate record of what is taking place here.'

'Have you asked them?'

'Of course, but like all journalists they are interested, not in the truth, but in news. They were frankly mystified; they probably thought I was trying to pull their legs.'

'You want me to change their perspectives?'

'Exactly. Do you think you can?'

'Possibly.' Maitland pointed to the walls around them. 'Are you sure this pyramid can stand up to the wind indefinitely?'

'Absolutely!' Hardoon scoffed. 'The walls are thirty feet thick; they'll carry the impact of a dozen hydrogen bombs. Five hundred miles an hour is a trivial speed. The paper-thin plating of aircraft fusilages withstands it comfortably.'

When Maitland seemed doubtful, Hardoon added: 'Believe me, Doctor, you need have no fears. This pyramid is completely separate from the old air-raid shelters. That is the whole point. The entire pyramid is above ground; there are no foundation members whatever. The shelters where you and the other personnel stay are two hundred yards away. This pyramid will withstand ten thousand-mile-an hour gales, a hundred thousand, if you can imagine such a speed. I am not joking. With the exception of this apartment the pyramid is a solid block of reinforced concrete weighing nearly twenty-five thousand tons, completely immovable, like the deep bunkers in Berlin which even high explosives could not destroy and which have remained where they were to this day.'

Hardoon waved to the guards waiting by the door.

'Kroll, Dr Maitland is ready to be shown to his quarters.' As the big guard ambled over to the desk, Hardoon looked up at Maitland. 'I think you understand me, Doctor. You are a man of science, accustomed to weighing evidence objectively. I put my case in your hands.'

'How long will we have to stay here?' Maitland asked.

'Until the wind subsides. A few weeks perhaps. Is it so important? You will find nowhere safer. Remember, Doctor, a footnote to history is being made here. Think in other categories, in a wider context.'

As he walked out with one of the guards, Maitland noticed that the shutters were retracting. Hardoon sat at his chair before the window, staring out as the thousand fragments of a disintegrating world soared past in a ceaseless bombardment. Just before the door closed behind Maitland the sounds of the wind rose up tumultuously.

From Hardoon's suite in the apex they took a small elevator down through the matrix of the pyramid to the communicating tunnel which ran to the bunker system 200 yards away. Maitland walked along the damp concrete uneasily, aware of the massive weight of the structure overhead, counting the dim lights strung along the tunnel.

He wondered whether there was any point in trying to

argue with Hardoon. But, as Hardoon had said, for the time being, the issue of personal freedom aside, there would be little point in trying to leave. Besides, Hardoon was probably ruthless. Not only did the behaviour of his armed guards indicate this, but unless he compelled their absolute loyalty the entire organization would have long since collapsed.

As they neared the midpoint of the tunnel the floor swayed slightly under their feet. Caught off balance, Maitland stumbled against the wall. The guard steadied him with one hand. Thanking him, Maitland noticed the expression on his face, a faint but nonetheless detectable hint of alarm.

'What's the matter?' Maitland asked him.

The guard, a tall, slim-faced boy with a light stubble under his helmet strap, scowled uneasily. 'What do you mean?'

Maitland paused. 'You looked worried.'

The guard eyed him balefully, watching for any suspicious move, then muttered obscurely. They walked on. The floor underfoot was an inch deep in water. Unmistakably, Maitland noticed, the tunnel walls were shifting.

'How deep down are we?' he asked.

'Fifty feet. Maybe less now.'

'You mean the subsoil's going? Good God, the wind will soon be stripping these bunkers down to their roofs.' The guard grunted at this. 'What's the subsoil here – clay?'

'No idea,' the guard said. 'Gravel, or something like that.'

'Gravel?' Maitland stopped.

'What's the matter with gravel?' the guard asked, his mouth fretting.

'Nothing in particular, except that it's pretty mobile.' Maitland pointed to the tunnel walls – they were now midway – and asked: 'Why's the tunnel leaking? The walls

168

are shifting around. They must be cracked somewhere.'

The guard shrugged. 'Wait till you see the bunkers. They're like a ship's bilge.'

'But the walls aren't actually moving, surely?' Maitland examined one of the hairline cracks high up on the ceiling. It widened as it neared the floor. Below their feet it was at least six inches broad, the opposing lips only held together by the net of reinforcing bars. Water seeped through steadily, fanning out across the cement.

'A couple of engineers from Construction were down here yesterday,' the guard confided. 'They were talking about the underground stream loosening the ground or something.'

'You'd better warn the old boy,' Maitland said. 'He's liable to be cut off if this tunnel fills up.'

'He'll be O.K. He's got everything he needs up there. Refrigerators full of food and water, his own generator.'

The guard looked uneasily along the tunnel. As they stepped through the tunnel and waited for Kroll to join them, Maitland glanced back and saw that the tunnel dipped sharply in the centre. The two sections inclined upward at an angle of two or three degrees.

With Kroll leading, occasionally stopping to shoulder Maitland ahead of him, they walked along a maze of corridors, stairways, and dimly lit ramps traversed by huge ventilator shafts and power cables. Generators charged continually, providing an unvarying background to the sounds of steel boots ringing on metal steps, voices bellowing orders. Now and then, through an open doorway, Maitland could see men in shirt sleeves slumped on trestle beds, crammed together among their gear in the minute cubicles.

They moved down a stairway towards the lowest level of the bunker system. Maitland estimated that at least 400 men were accommodated in the network of shelters, along with enough supplies to maintain them for six months. The corridors were lined with steel and wooden crates similar to the ones he had seen in Marshall's warehouse, overflowing from the big store chambers he had glimpsed on arrival.

Finally they emerged into the lowest level and entered a damp narrow cul-de-sac, at the end of which a couple of guards idled under a single light. They pulled themselves to attention as Kroll appeared and saluted him quickly, then unlocked a small door in the right-hand wall.

Kroll jerked his thumb at Maitland, bundled him brusquely through the doorway and slammed it behind him.

Maitland found the others inside, sitting on the beds around the wall, in the dull red gloom of a single storm bulb mounted over the door. Lanyon let out a low cheer when he saw Maitland, and helped him off with his jacket. Patricia Olsen lit him a cigarette, and Maitland stretched out gratefully on one of the hard horsehair mattresses.

'You've seen him, have you, Doctor?' Lanyon asked when Maitland had rested. 'He told you all about his moral stand against the hurricane?'

Maitland nodded, his eyes half closed with fatigue. 'The whole thing. He even showed me the wind tapping at his magic window. He's obviously out of his mind.'

'I'm not so sure,' Bill Waring, the other reporter, chipped in. He sat on his bed, pensively smoking a cigarette. 'In fact, his instinct of self-preservation may be stronger than we think. This is the most organized set-up I've come across. Three or four hundred trained men, half a dozen big vehicles, a radio station, agents all over the country – it's a really well-run military unit. The moral stand is probably just the sauce. I figure we ought to look ahead to the next stage, when the wind dies down and he finds he really can run the whole show if he wants to.'

Patricia Olsen, resting on another of the beds, nodded in agreement. 'He'll discover some other moral drive then, of course.' She shuddered, only half playfully. 'Can you just see friend Kroll as executive vice-president?'

Lanyon smiled at her. 'Relax. As long as Hardoon wants an attractive newswriter around you'll be safe.' He turned to Maitland, lowering his voice and glancing back at the door. 'Seriously, I've been trying to think up some way of getting us out of here.'

'I'm with you,' Maitland said. 'But how?'

'Well, I was just explaining to Pat and Bill that probably the quickest method is for them to play along with Hardoon, produce a highly coloured extravanganza about this lone hero outstaring the wind and so on. If he's sure we're sincere we can probably sell him on the idea that the story should be given a worldwide spread immediately.'

'To encourage everyone,' Bill Waring concluded. 'Help us keep our chins up. I agreed, it's the best bet.'

Pat Olsen nodded. 'We could easily do it. If he's got a cine camera around here we could even take some shots of him at his peephole.' She shook her head ruefully. 'My, oh my, but he really is a gone one.'

'Where are the radio operator and the driver?' Maitland asked.

'They joined the local forces,' Lanyon said. With a smile he added: 'Don't look so shocked; it's an established military tradition. Kroll even offered to make me corporal.'

For five days they remained sealed within the bunker. The doors into the corridor remained locked. Food was brought to them twice a day by two guards, but apart from an occasional routine check they were left virtually alone. The guards were curt and uncommunicative, and conveyed that some sort of activity was taking place on the upper levels which occupied most of the personnel for much of the day and night.

Their bunker was on the lowest level of the system, some two hundred feet below ground. The corridor led past a small wash-room to a spiral staircase which carried upward to the next level, and Maitland's impression was that a large

171

number of similar annexes had been built out off the main group of shelters.

The air, carried to them by a small ventilator, was damp and acrid, often mixed with the fumes of diesel engines, constantly varying in pressure from a powerful blast that chilled the room, spattering everything with an oily dust, to a low drift of warm air that made them sluggish and uncomfortable.

Maitland traced this to carbon-monoxide contamination, and asked one of the guards if he could check the inlet pipe, presumably mounted in the transport bays. But the man was unhelpful.

While Pat Olsen and Waring began to concoct their story of Hardoon's stand against the wind, Lanyon and Maitland did what they could to plan an escape. Maitland made several requests for an interview with Hardoon; nothing, however, came of this. Nor could he gain any news of Andrew Symington.

One thing they were spared – the monotonous drone of the wind. Deep in the bunker, they could hear nothing except the tap leaking in the washroom, the sounds of metal shoes slamming on the staircase above. Their energy dulled by the news that there was no sign of the wind's abatement – in fact, the speed had risen steeply now to 550 mph – they slumped about on the beds, half asleep, drugged by the carbon-monoxide fumes.

Waking some time after midnight, Maitland stirred, trying to return to sleep, then lay on his back in the thin red gloom of the storm bulb, listening to the sounds of his companions asleep. His bed was beside the door, with Lanyon at his feet, Waring and Pat Olsen along the far wall below the ventilator.

Outside in the corridor a few night sounds shifted through the darkness – steam pipes chuntering, orders being shouted,

172

freight loaded or unloaded in one of the storerooms on the next level.

Sometime later he woke again and found himself sweating uneasily. Everything around him was strangely quiet, the breathing of his companions obviously laboured.

Then he realized that the ventilator had stopped, its steady bellows-like action no longer overlaying the other noises in the bunker.

One sound alone stood out – the regular ping, ping, ping of a dripping tap, falling into a basin of water only a few feet away from him.

Inclining his head, Maitland suddenly saw the drip move through the air, the minute sparkle of light reflected in the red storm lamp.

Involuntarily, he sat up on one elbow, pushing away the tarpaulin square which served him as a blanket.

The drip was coming from the ventilator! The drops followed each other at half-second intervals, their rate of fall increasing as he listened.

Swinging his legs off the bed, he put his feet on the floor, then looked down in astonishment to see a wide pool of water almost reaching to his ankles.

'Lanyon! Waring!' he shouted. He leaped up as the others dragged themselves out of sleep, and pulled on his leather boots. Waring peered into the silent ventilator shaft, from which a steady trickle of water now emerged, pouring forward into the centre of the floor.

'There's no air coming through!' Waring shouted at the others. 'Must be a break somewhere up above.'

Lanyon and Maitland splashed over to the door and began to pound on the panels, shouting at the tops of their voices. Overhead, somewhere along the stairway, they could hear confused shouting, the sounds of feet running in all directions and of bulkheads being slammed.

Black, oil-stained water was pushing in a steady stream

173

below the door, reaching up the walls. Pat Olsen jumped up on Maitland's bed and crouched on the rail. Outside in the corridor the water appeared to be three or four inches deep, and was splashing noisily down the stairway. As Maitland and Lanyon heaved their shoulders against the steel door panels, the jet from the ventilator suddenly increased, throwing up a fountain that splashed across their backs.

Lanyon pulled Maitland away, pointed to one of the beds. 'Help me dismantle it! Maybe we can use the crossbars as jemmies.'

Quickly they pulled the mattress off the bed, ripped out the trestle and unlocked the two supporting bars, the heavy bolts ripping at their fingers. Freeing the angle irons, they forced the sharp ends into the narrow aperture between the door and the concrete wall, slowly levered the top half of the steel plate out of its louvers. As soon as it had sprung back a few inches, Lanyon reached up, seized the lip, and pulled it downward to provide a narrow, foot-deep opening.

Outside, in the corridor, only the red storm light was showing. As Lanyon began to scramble through the opening the light in their room went out, plunging them into a thin red gloom, the diffused rays from the bulb glimmering in the dark surface of the water.

It reached to Lanyon's knees in the corridor, pouring in a strong torrent down the stairway. Lanyon steadied himself, then helped Patricia Olsen through after him, followed by Waring and Maitland. As they left the room the water had reached the level of the beds, and two of the mattresses were sailing slowly around.

Quickly they waded down the corridor to the stairway, Lanyon leading. Water cascaded around their waists, and as they reached the first turning Maitland, who was last in line, looked back to see the surface only two feet from the ceiling.

Reaching the next level, they paused in a recess between

two corridors at right angles to each other. The influx of water was coursing down the right-hand section, pouring out through the shattered doorways of a series of high store chambers.

Lanyon pointed to their left, where half a dozen guards were piling sandbags across the corridor preparatory to sealing it with a heavy bulkhead.

'Hold on!' he shouted at them. 'Don't close up yet!'

He started to run towards them, but the guards ignored him. As Lanyon reached the bulkhead they slammed in the crossbars, leaving the American pounding helplessly on the massive grey plates.

Maitland straddled the sandbags, filled with a quick-setting cement which was already locking the breastwork to the floor and walls as the water swilled against it down the corridor. He held Lanyon's shoulder. 'Come on, let's make for the surface. No point in being trapped down here with these rats. There must have been a major cave-in somewhere. Once we get above it we'll be safe.'

Pulling themselves up the stairway, they made their way past the next two levels. Gradually the flow of water pouring past them diminished, and by the time they reached the top of the shaft it had stopped altogether. At each of the four levels the retreating occupants of the bunker system had sealed bulkheads across the corridors, blocking off the central redoubt on the left from the stairway and the flooded store chambers on its right.

Waring and Patricia Olsen sat down against the wall opposite the stairway, trying to squeeze the water out of their clothes, but Lanyon shouted at them: 'Come on, we can't stay here! If another of these walls goes the whole place will flood out. Our only chance is to get through into Hardoon's pyramid.'

One by one they entered the communicating tunnel, now in total darkness, guiding themselves along the walls. These were tilting, as if the tunnel were being twisted longitudinally. Water accumulated along the left-hand side, more than three inches deep. Tremendous faults had opened in the surrounding gravel bed, as the underground spring carried away enormous quantities of earth, leaving the massive bunkers suspended without support.

They reached the far end of the tunnel, made their way up a short stairway to the elevator shaft serving Hardoon's suite.

Lanyon turned to Waring. 'Bill, you stay down here with Pat, while Maitland and I see if we can reach Hardoon.'

He pulled back the cage of the elevator, made room inside for Maitland. He wiped his face with his sleeve, spitting out an oily phlegm that choked his sinuses, then pressed the tab marked 'Roof.'

Half-way up to the top the elevator suddenly swung back, lodged momentarily in its housings, banging against the rear wall of the shaft.

Lanyon stabbed the roof button again. 'Dammit, felt as if the whole place was moving,' he commented to Maitland.

'Impossible,' Maitland said. 'A five hundred-mile-an-hour gale would never shift this weight of concrete. Must have been some air driving up the shaft.'

The elevator creaked upward and finally stopped. Maitland pulled back the grille, found that the upper doors were open. They stepped out into the deserted hallway, where a light still shone over the reception desk in the corner.

As they neared the doors of Hardoon's office they heard the sound of the wind battering against the panels, and for a moment Maitland wondered whether the observation window in Hardoon's suite had been breached. Then he realized that the wooden doors in front of them would have been ripped off their hinges in a fraction of a second.

Lanyon nodded to him and they plunged through.

Inside the room the noise of the wind roared insanely in

their ears, louder than they had ever heard it. Unbroken and apparently at the heart of the maelstrom itself, it reverberated off the walls and ceiling like the wave front of some gigantic explosion. The force of the blast stunned the two men, and they stood uncertainly on the threshold, peering around for its source.

The room was in darkness, the sole illumination streaming in from the observation window. Standing in front of it, his face only a foot from the glass, was Hardoon, the flickering field of light playing across his granitic features like the flames of some cosmic hell. So completely involved was he with the wind that Maitland hesitated before stepping forward, as much held back by the intangible power of Hardoon's presence as by the sounds of the hurricane battering at the window.

Suddenly a second taller figure detached itself quickly from the darkness behind Hardoon, bent across the desk and pressed a button on the control panel.

Immediately the sounds dimmed and fell away, and the ceiling lights came on overhead. Hardoon looked over his shoulder in surprise. He pulled himself out of his reverie, and gestured impatiently at Kroll, who was covering Maitland and Lanyon with his .45.

Maitland called out: 'Hardoon! Listen, for God's sake! The bunkers are flooding, the foundations are caving in!'

Hardoon stared at him sightlessly, apparently unaware of Maitland's identity. His eyes focused uncertainly on the wall behind Maitland's head. Then he motioned again to Kroll with a snap of his fingers and turned back to the window.

'Hardoon!' Maitland shouted. He and Lanyon began to move forward, but Kroll leaped quickly around the desk, the large automatic holding them off.

'Turn around, both of you!' he snapped, pushing Maitland back with a heavy fist. They sidestepped out into the

177

hall, and Kroll closed the doors behind him. Flicking the barrel of the gun, he steered them into the elevator, then stood two yards away from them, left hand on the control switch, ready to close the doors, his right levelling the gun, first at Lanyon and then at Maitland.

'Kroll!' Maitland shouted. 'The shelters are collapsing! Four hundred men are trapped in there. You've got to get them across here.'

Kroll nodded coldly, his mouth tight, his eyes like black chisels under the visor of his helmet. He raised the barrel at Maitland's head, his jaw muscles tensing, bunching the skin into hard knots.

As his finger squeezed the trigger, Maitland dropped quickly to his knees, trying to avoid the bullet. He looked up, saw Kroll grunt and train the gun on him again. Lanyon had backed up against the side of the car, stabbed frantically at the control buttons.

Waiting for the bullet to crash into his skull, Maitland lowered his head.

Suddenly, without warning, the floor tipped sharply, knocking him against the side of the elevator. As he straightened himself he heard the .45 roar out, felt the bullet slam past his head into the leather padding, ripping a three-inch slash across it. Flung off his feet, Kroll lost his balance and tripped across the small table by the reception desk.

As he picked himself up, swearing in a low snarl, Maitland dived forward at the automatic held loosely in his hand. Above their heads the lights swung eerily, and the floor remained tilted at a slight angle.

'Lanyon!' Maitland shouted. 'Get his gun!'

Behind him, Lanyon dived out of the elevator and hurled himself onto Kroll.

As they staggered across the sloping floor, Lanyon slammed a heavy punch into Kroll's neck, pounding the big man with the full force of his weight. Kroll rolled with the blow,

178

holding off Maitland with his left arm, trying to free the automatic Maitland had seized with both hands.

For a moment they struggled tensely. Butting with his head, Kroll drove the heavy helmet up into Maitland's face. Maitland gasped for breath and sat down on the floor, grabbing Kroll's jacket with one hand and pulling the big man on top of him. Kroll pulled himself up onto his knees, sitting astride of Maitland, and knocked Maitland's hands away with a heavy left swing. As he rammed his forefinger into the trigger guard and levelled the automatic at Maitland's chest, Lanyon picked a massive glass ashtray off the reception desk beside them and brought the edge down across the narrow strip of exposed neck below Kroll's helmet.

The big man began to slump and Lanyon reached down and turned him by the shoulder and then slashed him again across the face with the ashtray, knocking his head backward onto the top of the desk, his face like an inflamed skull's.

'You've got him,' Maitland gasped. He stood up and staggered back against the wall and Kroll sank loosely onto his knees and then collapsed across the floor, blood running from a deep wound behind his ear onto the carpet. Maitland picked up the automatic, held the butt in both hands. 'God, that was close!'

Lanyon tried to find his balance on the angling floor. 'What the hell's happening here? The whole pyramid seems to be tipping over!'

The down light flashed in the indicator panel over the elevator.

'Warning!' Lanyon said. 'Come on, let's get out of here.'

'Wait a minute,' Maitland told him. Gripping the automatic carefully, he ran up the incline towards Hardoon's office.

The room was in darkness, the only light coming from

the observation window. Books had spilled from the high shelves and lay across the floor, chairs and tables had careened over to the far wall. Hardoon had been thrown heavily off balance, was pushing himself back to the window along the edge of the desk.

Maitland had started to move towards him when the floor tilted again, dropping an inch below his feet like a jerking elevator. He stumbled, saw Hardoon pitch sideways across the desk. Books cascaded from the shelves like toppling dominoes. Hardoon regained his footing, seized the window ledge with both hands and pulled himself back.

Maitland crossed to the desk, stepped around it and touched Hardoon on the shoulder. The millionaire looked back at him blindly, the flickering light outside illuminating his storm-riven features.

'Hardoon!' Maitland shouted. 'Get away from here!'

Hardoon shook him off, turned to the window. For a few seconds Maitland stared out at the scene below. The storm wind swept by at colossal speed, the dark clouds now and then breaking to reveal the dim outlines of the fortified shelters. The two long buttress walls had disappeared. In their place an enormous ravine, at least 100 feet deep, had opened in the ground, and a swift torrent of water emerged from the mouth of a huge rift and ran straight below the left-hand corner of the pyramid, carrying with it an ever-increasing load of debris swept from the exposed sides. On the extreme left, protruding out through the wall of the ravine, Maitland could see the sharp rectangular outlines of part of the main bunker system, the communications tunnel straddling the ravine like a bridge. Once fifty feet below ground, it was now completely exposed for almost a third of its length. Behind it were the square ledges and walls of other portions of the bunker, their unsupported weight wrenching huge cracks in their surface.

The floor tilted again, throwing the two men against each other. Maitland steadied himself, helped Hardoon back onto his feet. The older man clung forward at the window, holding it desperately.

'Hardoon!' Maitland shouted again. 'The entire pyramid is toppling! For God's sake get out while you can! Look down there and see for yourself, the foundations are being carried away.'

Hardoon ignored him. Eyes glazed, he stared obsessively into the night, watching the whirlwind of black air.

Maitland hesitated, then left him. As he crossed the room the floor sank abruptly and one of the bookshelves fell forward and crashed down across a chair. Maitland ducked past it, pausing at the door to look back for the last time at Hardoon. By now the angle of the floor was almost ten degrees, and the millionaire was staring upward into the sky like some Wagnerian super-hero in a beseiged Valhalla.

'Maitland!' Lanyon shouted angrily. He was standing by the elevator shaft, gesturing. On the floor beside him Kroll stirred slowly drawing his long legs together.

Maitland stepped quickly into the lift. 'We'll leave him here,' he said to Lanyon. 'Perhaps he can save Hardoon.' He stabbed the ground button, and the elevator slipped and then sank slowly down the shaft.

Waring and Patricia Olsen were crouching by the tunnel entrance as they stepped out, glancing up anxiously at the tilting ceiling.

'There's every chance that the whole pyramid will keel over,' Maitland said. 'Our best hope is to get back into the bunkers. Once the channel forces its way past the pyramid the shelters should drain again. Already they're well above the floor of the ravine.'

As they stepped back into the tunnel the pyramid jerked heavily, throwing them against the wall. Deep fissures had appeared in the cement. They ran along it, Maitland and Lanyon helping Patricia Olsen. Half-way down the tunnel they felt a second tremendous wrench that threw them onto their knees. Looking back, they saw a short section of the corridor buckle, its wall twisted like cardboard. At the same time, once again they heard the sound of the wind hammering past.

They reached the doorway at the far end. Inside, as Maitland had anticipated, the corridors had drained but the bulkheads were still sealed behind the breastwork.

As he looked back for the last time down the tunnel, Maitland saw the section twenty yards away abruptly rise up into the air like the limb of a drawbridge. For a moment there was a cascade of masonry and ruptured steelwork, and then the entire tunnel fell back to reveal a blinding sweep of daylight. Sucked out of the still intact section of tunnel attached to the bunker, air swept past Maitland under pressure, and he was dragged forward a dozen feet before he held himself against a step in one of the walls.

Through the open aperture he looked out into the huge ravine below, like the hundred-yard-wide trench working of a six-lane underpass. Dust and exploding gravel obscured its sides, bursting through the narrowing venturi, but he could see the great bulk of the pyramid towering overhead. The ravine led directly below it, but at least two-thirds of its base still rested on solid earth, the over-hanging portion revealing the L-piece of the communicating tunnel jutting below. The pyramid had tilted by a full ten degrees, snapping the tunnel in half like a straw.

Peering up, Maitland tried to identify the observation window in the apex, but it was hidden behind the dark clouds of detonating grit.

'Maitland!' he heard someone shout behind him, but he felt unable to tear his eyes from the spectacle before him. Like some enormous wounded mastodon, the pyramid reared up into the storm wind, the precarious shelf of ground on which it rested being cut away yard by yard as Maitland watched. The ravine deepened as the channel grew wider, now that the obstruction of the bunker system had been passed. For a few seconds the pyramid poised precariously, tipping slowly, apparently held by the adhesive forces of the ground below the small portion of its base still fastened to the supporting shelf.

Then, with a sudden final lurch, it toppled over the edge, and in a blinding explosion of dust and flying rock it fell sideways into the ravine. For a few moments its massive bulk rose over the clouds of debris, its apex pointed obliquely downward, resting on its left-hand face. Then the wind began to cover it, burying it completely beneath vast drifts of dust.

Stunned, Maitland gazed out at the scene of this cataclysmic convulsion. At his shoulder he found Lanyon, his arm around Patricia Olsen, with Waring behind them. Together they stared down into the ravine, watching the dust clouds pour past at incredible speed. Then numbly the little group withdrew along the short stump of tunnel and made its way into the corridor.

Waring and Patricia Olsen sat down on the top step of the stairway. Lanyon leaned against the wall, while Maitland squatted on the floor.

'I guess you've got your story, all right, Pat,' Lanyon said to the girl.

She nodded, pulling the hood of her jacket closer around her cold face. 'Yes, and maybe I can even believe it now. Just about the end to everything.'

'What do we do now, Commander?' Waring asked. 'We're not really much better off, are we? It's only a matter of hours before this place starts breaking up like a derelict wreck.'

Lanyon pulled himself together. On either side heavy bulkheads sealed the two corridors branching off from the stairway, huge cement-filled sandbags blocking their approach. He and Maitland examined the cracks appearing in the ceiling. Forced by their own weight, no longer supported by the surrounding earth, the bunkers were breaking apart. As Warning had said, soon the staircase and the segments of corridor would detach themselves and fall onto the floor of the ravine sixty feet below.

'I'll try the stairway,' Lanyon told the others. 'There's a chance we may be safer down below.'

Stepping past Pat Olsen, he began to make his way around, peering through the thin light. He had almost completed one circle when his foot plunged through the surface of a pool of water. Reaching down with his hands, he found that the stairwell was full. The three levels below had been completely flooded.

He rejoined the others. They had moved into the left-hand corridor, were pressed against the collapsing breastwork of sandbags. Maitland gestured Lanyon over quickly. Looking up, he saw that one of the cracks across the roof of the stairway was now two feet wide, a deep fissure in the thick concrete now widened perceptibly, moving in rigid jerks as the reinforcing bars snapped one by one like the teeth of a giant zip.

Suddenly, before he expected it, the entire corner section of the bunker containing the stairway and the recess between the corridors twisted and slid away into the ravine, sending up a tremendous cloud of white dust. A narrow projection of ceiling separated them from the open air stream, but above this was another toppling piece of masonry, a huge section of the original wall pivoting on its stem of reinforcing bars. Most of these had snapped, and the giant slab, a block weighing fifteen or twenty tons, was slowly tilting down over them.

Seeing it, Patricia Olsen began to scream helplessly, but Lanyon managed to steady her for a moment, looking around desperately for some way of escape. Their only chance seemed to be to slide down into the ravine, then hope they would find some narrow crevice where they could shelter from the monster poised above them.

Quickly he seized Patricia's arm, began to pull her towards the edge. She dug her heels in desperately, still clinging to the temporary safety of the ledge.

'No, Steve! Please, I can't!'

'Darling, you've got to!' Lanyon bellowed at her above the roar of the wind. He twisted her arm roughly, dragging her with him, holding the ragged ledge with his free hand before pushing her over.

'Lanyon! Wait!' Maitland grabbed his shoulder, then pulled Patricia back before she could fall. 'Look! Up there!'

They craned upward. Miraculously, the great wall section towering above them was slowly keeling backward away from them into the wind. Showers of stones and flying pieces of rubble cascaded across its exposed surface, but by some extraordinary reversal of the laws of nature, it was no longer yielding to the greater force of the wind.

Amazed, they looked up at this incredible defiance, intervening like some act of God to save them.

Suddenly Maitland shouted out into the air, began to pound insanely on the wall of the ledge. For a moment he raged away hysterically, and then Lanyon and Waring held his arms and tried to calm him.

'Hold it, Doctor,' Lanyon roared into his face. 'Don't be a fool. Control yourself!'

Maitland shook himself free. 'Look, Lanyon, up there! Don't you realize what's happened, why that wall fell away from us, *into* the wind? Don't you see?' When they frowned at him in bewilderment he shouted, '*The wind's dropping! It's finally spent itself!*'

Sure enough, the great fragment of wall was moving slowly forward into the face of the wind. Maitland pointed at the sky around them. 'The air's lighter already! The wind's dying down, you can hear it. It's finally subsiding!'

Together they looked across the ravine. As Maitland had said, visibility had now increased to over 600 yards. They could see plainly across the black fields beyond the estate, even trace the remains of a road winding along the periphery. The sky itself had lightened, was now an overcast grey, the sweeping pathways across it inclined slightly downward.

Like a cosmic carousel nearing the end of its run, the storm wind was slowly losing speed.

More about Penguins and Pelicans

Penguinews, which appears every month, contains details of all the new books issued by Penguins as they are published. From time to time it is supplemented by *Penguins in Print*, which is a complete list of all available books published by Penguins. (There are well over four thousand of these.)

A specimen copy of *Penguinews* will be sent to you free on request. For a year's issues (including the complete lists) please send 30p if you live in the United Kingdom, or 60p if you live elsewhere. Just write to Dept EP, Penguin Books Ltd, Harmondsworth, Middlesex, enclosing a cheque or postal order, and your name will be added to the mailing list.

Note: *Penguinews* and *Penguins in Print* are not available in the U.S.A. or Canada

The Penguin Science Fiction Omnibus

Edited by Brian Aldiss

The biggest, most exciting collection of science fiction stories ever! Including stories from such masters as Harry Harrison, Isaac Asimov, Frederik Pohl, Arthur C. Clarke, C. M. Kornbluth, James Blish, Clifford Simak, J. G. Ballard and many more . . . Selected and introduced by Brian Aldiss

Cat's Cradle

Kurt Vonnegut

The strange story of *ice-nine* and what happened when the stuff got loose.

Make Room! Make Room!

Harry Harrison

In a city of 35 million people, living on lentils, soya beans and – if they're lucky – the odd starving rat, Andy Rush is engaged in a desperate and lonely hunt for a killer everyone has forgotten. Now filmed as *Soylent Green*.

The Three Stigmata of Palmer Eldritch

Philip K. Dick

On the barren sister planets of Earth, Can D, superdrug, offers the drafted colonists their only form of escape – and gives Earth its most valuable export. Then Palmer Eldritch and Chew Z arrive on the scene from another system. Chew Z – the ultimate drug of all time, transforming, transporting and timeless. This is Philip K. Dick at his hallucinatory best.

Apeman, Spaceman

Edited by Leon E. Stover and Harry Harrison with a foreword by Carleton S. Coon

What if Homo Sapiens was just a rather special breed of galactic wild rabbit? Or a high class form of goldfish – Homo-Piscis? What if he were spiritually inferior to a resurrected version of Neanderthal Man – who can even beat him at American football?

Apeman, Spaceman is a collection of anthropological SF stories which all pose the question: what is man's place in the Universe? To someone, somewhere, we are inferior, perhaps even unnoticeable, and yet here we are teaching dolphins cheap tricks. But one day . . .

Not for sale in the U.S.A. or Canada

The Space Merchants

Frederik Pohl and C. M. Kornbluth

Time: a hundred years hence. Place: Madison Avenue, New York. An overcrowded world is dominated by giant advertising agencies which do not stop short of armed warfare in their struggles with one another. The President has become a puppet, and the rest of the world has been reduced to the status of drug-and-ad-conditioned helots.

'Has many claims to being the best science fiction novel so far' – Kingsley Amis in *New Maps of Hell*

Not for sale in U.S.A. or Canada

The Terminal Beach

The crystal world of J. G. Ballard where the white light of reason bends and breaks into every shade of fear . . . Twelve chill splinters of unreality.

The Drought

Rain is a thing of the past. Radio-active waste has stopped the sea evaporating. The sun beats down on the parching earth, and on the parching spirit of man. A warped new humankind is bred out of the dead land – bitter, murderous, its values turned upside-down. Idiots reign. Water replaces currency and becomes the source of a bleak new evil . . .

The Drowned World

'Ballard is one of the brightest new stars in post-war fiction. This tale of strange and terrible adventure in a world of steaming jungles has an oppressive power reminiscent of Conrad' – Kingsley Amis.

Not for sale in the U.S.A.